W9-CAW-696

NAVAJO

SUMMER

NAVAJO

SUMMER

Jennifer Owings Dewey

with drawings by the author

Boyds Mills Press

Acknowledgments

Thanks to E. Wendy Saul for thoughtful, wise, and tireless assistance during the revision of this manuscript. Thanks, also, to the Wilson family—for taking me in and allowing me to share their lives.

Copyright © 1998 by Jennifer Owings Dewey
All rights reserved

Published by Caroline House
Boyds Mills Press, Inc.
A Highlights Company
815 Church Street
Honesdale, Pennsylvania 18431
Printed in the United States of America

Publisher Cataloging-in-Publication Data
Dewey, Jennifer Owings.
    Navajo Summer / by Jennifer Owings Dewey.—1st ed.
[144]p. : ill. ; cm.
Summary:This story of a young girl who runs away from home to live with a Navajo family is based on the author's childhood.
ISBN 1-56397-248-4
1. Runaways—Fiction—Juvenile literature. 2. Navajo Indians—Juvenile Fiction.
3. Summer—Fiction—Juvenile literature [1. Runaways—Fiction.
2. Navajo Indians—Fiction. 3. Summer— Fiction.] I.Title.
813.54 [F]—dc20   1998   AC   CIP
Library of Congress Catalog Card Number 97-72770

First edition, 1998
Book designed by Tim Gillner
The text of this book is set in 12-point Garamond Book
The drawings are done in pencil.

10 9 8 7 6 5 4 3 2 1

To the Navajo People
—J. O. D.

Contents

A Note about Rock Art

The Indian rock art images used to decorate this book are from western Colorado, the Colorado Plateau, and the Rocky Mountains.

For more than five thousand years, this vast geographical area was populated by hunters and gatherers, nomads who roamed the region in seasonal cycles. Evidence of their existence is revealed to us in mysterious paintings and etchings found on rocks and sandstone walls.

The images seem to describe connections and relationships between prehistoric human beings and the natural world, including celestial events. The Navajo People, relative late-comers compared to the Anasazi, were Athabaskan tribes that migrated from the far north and settled, eventually, in the region that is now Arizona and New Mexico. Their rock art describes more modern themes: encounters with Spanish horsemen, for example, and trains riding on steel rails.

It is not possible to know the exact meanings of rock art images. Present-day cultures are thousands of years removed from those ancient times. We can only guess, and use our imaginations.

NAVAJO
SUMMER

In the summer of 1953 I was twelve years old. It was a summer of great change. Afterward, nothing was the same for me. *Navajo Summer* is a story based on my memories of that time . . . .

ARIZONA

CANYON de CHELLY

CHINLE

WILSON HOME

WINDOW ROCK

GALLUP

UTAH   COLORADO

ARIZONA   NEW
             MEXICO

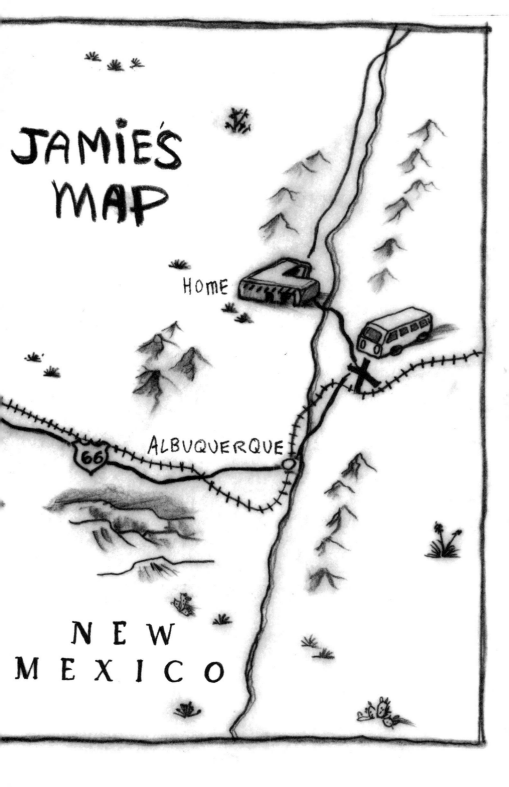

ON THE BUS

I got on the bus before anybody else. Other passengers began to come aboard. I watched them, a steady stream of people. Most of them were Navajo. I was in a window seat near the back on the right side.

Mothers climbed the bus steps, shifting the weight of babies held close against their shoulders. Broad hands shielded the wrapped bundles protectively. Eyes flashed in the haze inside the bus. It took time, I knew, to get used to the shadowy gloom after the daylight outside.

I had an imaginary map fixed in my mind, a map that showed where I was going. Black lines marked a white background, with an X for the bus station, another X for Window Rock, and another for the Canyon—my final destination.

People touched the bus seats hesitantly before sitting down, squeezing and patting the cushions with their fingers as if to test the softness. Older children tugged gently on the arms and wrists of smaller ones, urging them along.

No voices were raised. There wasn't any scolding or ordering around—like I was used to at home.

My little brother had been sleeping when I left. He was still a baby, young enough for naps. By now he'd be awake and running around. It was past four in the afternoon. His white-blond hair would be sticking straight up, the way it always did when he had been sleeping.

I pushed the thought of him out of my mind, making room for my imaginary map, the one with the X's on it. I had escaped. I was free. I was moving further from my family with every breath.

Passengers struggled to stow luggage. They had cloth bags and blanket rolls; some carried paper sacks with string handles. They set their belongings on metal racks overhead and took seats.

One girl, who might have been my age, twisted around to stare at me. I caught her eyes. They were large, dark, and shiny. She didn't smile before turning her face away. I knew she was curious. I was the only white child on the bus, and I was traveling alone besides.

Hushed rhythms of conversation were muffled by the heavy atmosphere in the bus. I strained, trying to hear, to make out words spoken in quiet voices. I was certain the friendly murmurings would help me feel less alone.

It didn't work that way. I felt worse because I was

eavesdropping. I shut my eyes and pretended the people were not human after all—they were insects, bees, wasps, and beetles. The humming sounded the way insects do in trees and bushes, like a swarm of tiny animals buzzing and clicking, not like people with personal things to say to each other.

Edna and Bill would be the first to notice that I was gone. But not yet. It was still early. They knew I sometimes stayed out until after supper, sometimes until after the dishes were done and put away.

I rubbed the empty bus seat next to me, one of the few left after everybody settled down. The fabric was warm and rough under my hand. Even though I didn't want to talk to a stranger, the vacant seat made me afraid that people would notice I was traveling alone.

The air was stuffy and hot. I felt sick. I knew there was no place to throw up, except in the bathroom back inside the station.

I stayed in my seat. I would not run to the bathroom. If I left, the bus would drive off without me. I'd be stuck in the station, feeling dumb and desperate.

Instead I concentrated on the flies banging against the window glass. At home, in the kitchen, flies crashed into the windows. Edna hated them. She'd go after them like a crazy woman, swatting them with her swatter, a yellow plastic one—she would miss every time. The flies just ended up dying on the sills, needing to be scooped up and thrown away later.

A small silver fan was attached to the front of the bus, over the dashboard above the driver's seat. It wasn't turned on. A shiny piece of mesh covered the front of it, like a fencer's mask. I longed for our driver to come and turn the fan on. I'd be sick if he didn't come soon.

I'd been staring at two bus drivers through the window. They were standing on the concrete platform under the shade of an overhang. They smoked cigarettes and talked. Both men wore gray pants, gray shirts, and gray caps with visors. I knew which driver was ours. He kept touching the side of the bus with his hand, in an almost tender way.

I took a long, deep breath when our driver dropped his cigarette and rubbed it into the ground with his shoe. He climbed aboard the bus, swinging up the steps, taking two at a time.

The door closed with a sucking sound. "You can't change your mind now," I whispered to myself, remembering the map in my mind.

I held tightly to the bottom of my seat, wondering why the bus company used scratchy, uncomfortable fabric to cover its seats. Every time my legs rubbed against it, my bare skin itched.

The driver moved slowly up the aisle. I tried to see his eyes but they were hidden under the bill of his cap. He tore stubs off the passengers' tickets with his fingers. His fingers were fat, with clipped-back nails. He greeted passengers in a way my mother would have hated. He was friendly and informal, talking easily to people. Around someone like him, my mother would lift her shoulders and turn her face away, not smiling.

The driver's voice was close enough that I could make out words, even whole sentences. He was asking people where they were going, what their final destinations were. He spoke with a Texas twang like Bill's.

Bill was the wrangler on our ranch, the boss of the other ranch hands, and the one person, besides my father, who made important decisions about the animals and crops. Bill was originally from Texas. He talked with a drawl. Edna, Bill's wife, came from Texas Hill Country, too. Her accent was even thicker than Bill's. Bill and Edna were the people I'd miss the most once I got to the last X on my map.

I watched the driver approaching and felt panic rise in my throat. Would he know I was a runaway and throw me off the bus? He couldn't tell anything from looking at me, not if I acted normal, like everybody else.

I unhooked my fingers from the seat bottom and handed the driver my ticket. He took it just like the others, ripping it into two halves and giving me the smaller piece to keep.

"Going to Window Rock, are you?" he asked, holding his part of the stub.

"Yes," I said.

"You're on the right bus then, young lady."

He nodded and smiled. He moved to the next passenger. I was just another traveler in his eyes—a twelve-year-old with a paid-for ticket in her hand.

Tears of relief came, wet and warm under my eyelids. I pressed my face against the window.

The sun set. My face stared back at me, reflected in the glass.

We took Highway 66, a two-lane paved road going west toward Navajo Country. The highway was smooth and even, a gray stream with a yellow line down the middle. It stretched out the way a ribbon does when it flies through the air, mysterious and exciting.

I wanted to keep a vigil, to peer at the world outside the window and make sure we were on the road heading west every minute. I didn't dare take my eyes off the telephone poles whizzing by, their strings of wires dipping and rising with the speed of light.

By now my family would know I was missing from home. They'd be calling Martha, my best friend, to ask questions. They'd talk to Martha's mother and father. Martha's mother would worry that I'd been kidnapped. She was like that, always worrying about things that never happened in our valley.

My mother wouldn't know what to think or to say, much less what to do. She'd cry quietly, almost without sound. My father would yell. He'd be more furious with me now than ever. I got cold remembering his face, the way it would get swollen and red with rage. Daddy would often lose control and burst into noisy anger, scaring my mother and twin sisters and terrifying my little brother.

They'd all be shocked and amazed that I ran away, but the feeling of relief I had, escaping from them, was greater than my worry over what their reaction might be.

I had been on the road west before, traveling with Bill when he went to buy horses.

I had also been to Navajo Country with my father. He would often tell Mother I'd be the one going with him, not the other kids. Mother would nod her agreement, eyes down. I never wanted to go with him. I hated his unpredictable anger. He turned into a madman and yelled and scolded over nothing. He drove the truck too fast and risked our necks. Mother never said no to him, even when I pleaded with tears in my eyes.

My father took me a lot of places, just me alone. He called me his special child. I never knew why he said this. I did not have the courage to ask. It took half a second for him to go from being silent and brooding to lashing out and hitting me across the face or smacking me on the shoulder. If I cried, he jeered at me. Most of the time I was able to hide my feelings.

When the moon came up, I could see the mountain ranges outlined against the sky. They were humped like the backs of sleeping animals. I could also see the salt flats, shimmery and white in the moonlight. Bill told me the flats had been lakes millions of years ago; now not even a blade of grass would grow there.

The surface of the desert outside the window resembled the texture of cowhides I'd seen Bill stretch. He would take a hide, still wet after the slaughter of a cow, and nail it to a wooden frame, hammering it down along the edges and leaving it to dry in the heat of the sun. The desert, like the hides, got baked and bleached until the land looked ready to blow away in the wind. It was scabby and dry and bumpy, with clumps of sagebrush that looked like tufts of hair.

I loved the desert landscape. It was familiar to me the way a friend is, someone you've known so long you can't remember not knowing the person.

I'd left home with all my money in my pocket—every saved-up cent. I had walked away from the house in the late afternoon, after my last fight with Daddy, when everything was quiet under the cottonwood trees.

I had no plan for getting to any of the X's on my mental map, not even the first one, which was the bus station in town. I figured it would be a long, hot walk. I was just lucky that Mrs. Gonzales, a near neighbor of ours, saw me and offered me a ride.

Mrs. Gonzales was probably in her late thirties, but she had the sharp bones and dry skin of someone much older. Her false teeth gleamed and shone in her mouth as if they'd been made and put in the day before.

She never asked questions the way some adults did. As she drove, she just told me it was nice to have company on her way into town. But her eye did latch onto my knapsack, which was crammed full.

"You taking a trip? Got your bag all packed?" she asked, but she never waited for an answer. I smiled, nodding, and that was all she said.

She talked about her grocery list and how she hoped to get the food items she needed in town. "It's a long drive for nothing if they don't have what you want," she told me.

It was steamy and airless in the old Ford coupe Mrs. Gonzales drove. I rolled down my window, making it hard to hear her conversation.

She said her husband took the truck, the vehicle with good seats and a dashboard fan.

"He has a bad back," she explained.

I knew about the bad back. Everybody in the valley knew. Mr. Gonzales used to work in construction. He had fallen off a bridge, so he was on disability. He was a big person. All he did now was sit around like a lump in his overalls, or drive his truck up and down the dirt road.

Mrs. Gonzales dropped me off at the bus station and waved good-bye as if she'd be seeing me in a day or two.

I knew she wouldn't tell my parents about giving me a ride. They never spoke to her unless there was a handyman job my father wanted Mr. Gonzales to do. "They're not our kind," my mother would say.

The good luck I had in meeting up with Mrs. Gonzales continued.

The ticket to Window Rock, a town in Arizona, was only eight dollars. I had twenty-three dollars with me, which was more than enough. No one asked why I was traveling alone, or why I wanted just a one-way ticket.

The driver kept the bus running at high speeds all night, even on the curves. I kept a steady watch on the world outside the window. I saw the lights of trucks and cars loom up behind, then swing around, then pass and disappear. Those people probably had to get somewhere: a job in a new town, a destination with a cargo that couldn't wait. They could not afford to take time to rest. Like me, they had to remain alert, wide awake, and watchful every minute.

I tried to imagine what it was like to drive a car across the desert alone at night, or to drive a trailer truck from Austin to Los Angeles. It must make a person feel all alone in the universe, taking a trip like that.

One of my favorite things to do at night at home was to sit with Bill and Edna in the kitchen after supper and listen to the radio. This could only happen when Mother and Daddy were away from home. Edna didn't mind if I lost sleep by staying up late to listen to the country radio station. She liked it as much as I did.

I especially loved gospel music, which was scratchy and hard to hear because it came from distant towns in Oklahoma and Texas, places I'd never seen and couldn't even imagine. I'd float into the music, swimming with the chords as if I were adrift in warm water, feeling loose and peaceful.

Sometimes I'd tell Bill and Edna the eerie feelings I had about people who had to stay up all night. Those people must be lonely and sad, unlike the people who slept at night and stayed awake in the daytime. I thought maybe those people found comfort in listening to country stations, the same way we did. I believed music from faraway places surely made them feel better.

Bill and Edna owned the only radio we had on the ranch. It was a brown plastic box with a cloth that covered the speaker. Their radio smelled of burning wires; I loved that smell. Tuning in at night meant you got more distant stations than you got in the daytime. I never figured out why that was true, but it was.

If my parents were away, Bill and Edna took my sisters and brother and I to town on supply trips. We'd stop for lunch at Bill's favorite hamburger joint, which had a jukebox. The machine was as tall as me, wide, fat, and covered with chrome. It looked like a car had been parked off to one side of the room. The arm moved slowly, like an insect's leg, picking up records and dropping them on a silver platter.

I must have dozed then, thinking about Bill, Edna, and country music on the radio, because I woke up sweating from a bad dream. The bus gears were grinding and the brakes were gasping. We'd arrived in Gallup, New Mexico, the first stop on the way to Window Rock.

A handful of passengers stirred. They gathered belongings and sleeping children, shaking the young ones gently to wake them. They got off, slowly and silently, and filed into the glare of the station.

I was sad to see them go. New people got on, but I missed the old ones. They were people I didn't even know. How could I miss them?

The driver came up the aisle, as he'd done before, tearing off stubs and making marks for each person on a piece of paper attached to his clipboard. I smelled cigarette smoke coming off his clothes. This time he was quiet, not talking like before. I pretended to be asleep when he came past me.

The bus heaved out of the station, fuming and stinking with exhaust smoke, and turned sharply to the left. We passed through the rest of town on the main street, traveling alongside the railroad tracks.

A freight train clicked and clattered along the rails, going in the same direction as the bus. It moved like a caterpillar on a branch, gently swaying, slowly and easily. The train's whistle whined, a long, drawn-out moan—a wail. The sound was as weary and sad as any I'd ever heard.

The lights of Gallup blinked, flickered, and were finally snuffed out by darkness and distance. The freight curved away on the rails and disappeared from view. The echo of its whistle was still in my head. I loved the sound even though it was sad. It was plaintive and yearning, reminding me of my favorite country songs.

The freight train seemed alive, like a living thing, a beast with a brain and feelings. I wondered if hobos rode that train and slept in their clothes on boxcar floors. They were men with no place to go, who spent their lives drifting. My father was gone a lot, traveling, but he was no drifter. He always came back home to torment us.

Bill had told me about hobos. He explained that some of them might have had homes once, even wives and children, but they didn't want to go back. Maybe there was something wrong in their heads, Bill said, that kept them away from home.

I wondered if I could ever be like that—a person who moved all the time, with a home somewhere I never went to?

Bill had an uncle—a true-blue hobo—who rode the rails. I thought it was exciting to know someone with a hobo in the family. But Bill didn't think highly of drifters, and he wouldn't say much about his uncle. When I asked him why, he looked at me funny.

"It's best when a person finds a place to belong and stays put. If he sticks with a place, and doesn't give up, nobody can take it from him. Drifting doesn't lead to anything but grief."

Every person needed to have a safe place picked out to go home to. Bill was right.

But Bill's talk about a piece of ground you called your own, the stake he put on it, bothered me. He didn't have anything solid to call his own. I pictured forty acres and a stream for him. Bill would have horses, and some cows. There'd be chickens—Edna loved chickens—and fresh eggs for breakfast.

But Bill worked for my father. Daddy was mean and

stingy with hired people. When I asked Bill why he kept working for Daddy, he said he stayed on for our sakes. Then he'd say, "I have a retirement agreement with your dad. When the time comes that I'm too old to rope a steer or break a horse, your dad promises to settle some money on Edna and me. Meanwhile, we stay because of you kids. It's like raising our own bunch, having you around."

Bill wouldn't give me details about the agreement. I knew only that it existed, but I felt safer knowing about their deal. It made it less likely that Bill and Edna would suddenly pack up and leave one day.

Bill was the one person, along with Edna, who would figure out why I had picked the place I did for running to. I could see his face in my mind. I pictured his half-smile, the expression he wore when he knew and understood something.

He would never tell me the details of his life or Edna's life before they came to work for my father. I wanted to know about their lives because I was afraid they would want to leave and find better jobs somewhere else. Most people would have gotten fed up pretty quickly with the way Daddy treated them.

I let Bill and Edna know, through certain things I said and did, that I didn't want them to leave, not ever. I wanted them to stay until I was grown up and ready to move away myself.

Edna would tell me, "Don't you worry. We like it here just fine. We're not going anywhere anytime soon."

My mother said it was rude to pry into other people's business. To me, it didn't seem like prying if it was your friend you were asking, if it was someone you cared about as much as you cared about yourself.

After Gallup we made stops in small towns where a handful of lights shone under a huge dark sky filled with stars. There was dust in the air, and the bus stayed hot, even though the fan in front ran all night long.

Then I must have slept, because I was jerked awake when we rolled into Window Rock at seven the next morning.

At the Wilsons'

I stood outside the bus station, feeling the heat beginning to rise off the pavement, and wondered how to get the rest of the way. I'd followed a Navajo family getting off the bus. Now they stood close to me—a father, a mother, and four children. There were two girls and two boys. A pair of young Navajo men greeted the family. All of them moved toward a pickup truck parked at the curb.

"Could I hitch a ride?" I asked.

The father glanced at me, then he looked aside. "Depends," he said. When a Navajo doesn't know you, he or she won't look you in the eyes. It's considered rude. "Where you headed?"

"Chinle," I answered, realizing that I had asked for a ride before knowing where the family was going.

"We're going that way," the man said, with his eyes on the door panel of the truck. "Hop in. We have room."

The rest of the family and the two young men seemed to agree to include me. Nobody looked at me directly.

The father was dressed in a familiar way. The style was loosely adapted from the clothes of the first white people the Navajo ever saw—pioneer traders who came to the area when white people were first moving west. The man wore tight-fitting denim jeans, a long-sleeved red velvet shirt open at the neck, a silver concho belt with a shiny buckle, a silver wrist guard, a black felt hat, and moccasins. Turquoise earrings dangled from holes in his ears, and a heavy silver necklace was draped around his neck. His long black hair was caught up in a "chongo," a loop tied with yarn.

The Navajo woman and her two little girls were also traditionally dressed in cotton skirts that fell to their ankles and were held close to their waists with broad, woven belts. Their blouses were identical: dark blue cotton with long sleeves, buttoned at the neck. Around their heads the two girls wore scarves that were neatly tied under their chins. Their hair, which hung loose in smooth waves down their backs, caught the sun's light when they moved.

The two young boys and the young men wore denim jeans. Instead of the traditional long-sleeved cotton shirts, they had on white T-shirts, the kind you can buy at JC Penney. Seeing them in their modern clothes made me feel less conspicuous in my dirty blue jeans and faded cotton cowboy shirt.

The pickup bed was lined with cotton blankets and woolen rugs layered on top of each other. Brown paper sacks of groceries were stashed up against the cab to keep them out of the wind and dust.

Then the people climbed in. I was with the kids and the young men in the back; the adults were in front.

We left town. I looked back to catch a glimpse of the sandstone bridge that Window Rock had been named for. It was an arch of red rock with a hole in it. The sky shone brightly through the hole like a staring blue eye.

Our ride took us over rough dirt roads that led into the heart of Navajoland. We traveled further from the main highway with every bumpy mile.

We stopped along the way so that everyone could relieve themselves. On one of these stops the father told me his name was Bennie Shay. He wanted to know who I was going to see.

"The Wilsons," I answered. My voice sounded funny, and I realized I hadn't spoken since yesterday. "My father and my father's foreman trade with David Wilson Sr. for horses. I've been to visit them lots of times." Suddenly my words were a flood pouring from my throat. "We get most of our horses from them. I've been going to Chinle ever since I was five. That's when I first met the Wilsons, when I was five." The torrent stopped. I didn't know what else to say.

Mr. Shay looked right into my eyes. I could see the thoughts turning in his head, his doubts and questions about an Anglo girl traveling alone to Chinle. "I see," he said quietly.

His dark, handsome face was without expression, almost solemn. He said nothing further. He just nodded and turned, showing with a wave of his hand that it was time to get going again.

When we drove into Chinle, it was lit with a scattering of miniature lights that looked like shiny beads dropped on a dark cloth. It was well past sunset.

The wind was blowing hard. My face was coated with grit; my mouth was full of it. As I rubbed my eyes, I was aware of dirt, sweat, a terrible weariness, and hunger. I told myself to stay alert. "It won't be long now," I whispered to myself.

"We know the Wilsons," Mr. Shay yelled out the truck window. "We'll drop you there. Do they know you're coming?"

"No," I answered truthfully. "Not exactly."

"I hope they're home," Mr. Shay called back, shouting into the wind.

I hoped so, too. I pictured my map with the X's on it. I was getting near the last one, the final X—the Canyon.

Dust and trash were swirling around in clouds along the dirt streets of Chinle. The wind seemed to be alive, with a mind of its own. I remembered how the Navajo feel about the wind that turns against the spin of the earth. To a Navajo this kind of wind is a bad thing, a dark omen.

Luckily for me, the Wilsons' house lights were on. They were home. I don't know what I would have done if they'd been gone, with their house dark and empty.

The Shay family dropped me off in the yard and drove away. I went to the front door of the house and knocked. The door opened, and Dora, the mother, looked at me as if I were a ghost. I could tell she thought she was imagining things, seeing me standing there. Nervous seconds passed before she smiled and reached out with both hands to draw me in.

I heard Mr. Wilson say, from somewhere inside the house, "Who is it, Dora? Who's coming around this time of night?"

I was greeted warmly, with hugs, handshakes, and an obvious yet wordless surprise. Among the Navajo it is considered rude to ask a visitor questions when he or she first arrives, no matter how unexpected the visit might be. Watching the faces circling me, the curious eyes and smiling mouths, I knew their questions would come in time.

I couldn't help but eye chunks of fry bread on the table. I was hurriedly offered some, and then shown where to wash. I was handed a clean towel so I could dry off. Dora escorted me to bed. Her expression was quizzical, her mouth firm. I knew I would be questioned in the morning, after I'd had a much needed rest. I fell into bed, too tired to think.

Morning came with a sunlit stillness. Before I opened my eyes I knew there was no wind or blowing dust like there had been the night before.

When everybody was awake and sitting around the table, I could see they were ready to hear my story. It was plain from the looks on their faces and their sidelong glances, which were expectant and curious. The whole clan was present: David Wilson Sr., a man of about fifty; his oldest son, David Wilson Jr.; Dora, David Sr.'s wife; and the Wilsons' six other children. Dora put her hand on my shoulder and poured me a cup of black coffee.

"How did you get here?" Mr. Wilson asked. "Before you met up with the Shays?"

I was about to say "On the bus," when one of the younger children said, "Did your parents die?"

"No, they're getting a divorce," I said. I looked across the table to find David Wilson Sr.'s eyes resting intently on my face. I wanted to tell them about everything—the argument with my father, running to my room afterward, the betrayal I had felt in those moments, and my father's lie. But I wanted them to know instantly, without me having to describe it in painful, agonizing detail. Then they would understand, plain as day, that I had no choice but to run away.

"Can you say what happened," Mr. Wilson asked gently, "that made you leave home and come here like this?"

"Daddy is selling the ranch. Bill and Edna are going back to Texas. I asked them to take me, too. Daddy fired them. Everybody has to leave. Bill said after they get settled, when Edna and him have jobs and a place to live, I can visit, maybe even stay."

Dora brought out a platter of pan-fried potatoes and tortillas. This was the morning meal. Forks began to clatter against ceramic plates. There was quiet while the family ate. I was grateful for the pause in conversation. I felt the urge to blurt out everything but I couldn't seem to find the words to say anything.

Dora kept getting up and going into the kitchen and coming back with more food—eggs and bacon, a gallon-sized container of iced tea for those who didn't want coffee. The oldest Wilson daughter, Linda, poured the honey-colored liquid into blue plastic glasses. My hunger was more real than my need to speak. I ate everything on my plate and then asked for more.

When the meal was nearly finished, Linda gave me a long look. She said, "Tell us what happened."

I scanned the faces around the table. All eyes were on me. I couldn't stall any more.

"Daddy called us into his office, the one he has at the back of the house. He asked us, my sisters and me, who we wanted to live with."

I stopped talking and swallowed hard, feeling tears coming. I put a bite of food into my mouth. They were all paying close attention to each word I spoke. I wondered if I could tell them enough to make them understand my true reasons for leaving home.

"Go on," Dora said softly. "The rest?"

"He asked me where I wanted to live, as if I could really choose. I said 'On the ranch, or with Edna and Bill.' Then he started into one of his rages. He said I had to go where he told me. . . . First he said I could choose. Then he changed his mind. He said I had to live with my mother and the man she's going to marry. He slapped me hard across the face when I said 'Let me stay here, or live with Bill and Edna.' That's all."

"Not quite all?" David Sr. suggested.

"My mother wouldn't even talk to me. She was in her room crying. My sisters don't care about leaving the ranch. They told me so."

It sounded simple, the way the words came out of my mouth. Did they know how afraid I was of my father? They couldn't know how he bullied and raged, how he found reasons to use his belt on me when all I did was walk into a room where he happened to be. They'd never seen the cruel side of him, the side that took pleasure in humiliating me.

One time he came home with a new saddle just for me.

It wasn't my birthday. There was no occasion for the gift. It was the most beautiful saddle I'd ever seen. Daddy smiled at my obvious pleasure and said, "Go saddle soap it. That's what you do with new saddles."

I started in, and after about four hours of rubbing I decided the saddle was done. It was satiny soft with fresh layers of soap.

"It's not done," he said, looming over me where I sat on the tack room floor. My hands and arms were lathered with saddle soap. "Needs more."

I set to work again. That was when it dawned on me that he'd make me work that saddle until he was good and ready to let me stop, no matter how finished it was. This was the price I paid for his "gift."

I worked on the saddle all day and well into night. I missed supper. The moon was up and everybody was asleep when he finally came and told me to get up and go to bed.

Daddy was like that. Nothing I ever did seemed to make him change.

The day I left, everything had happened with sickening suddenness—the fight when I "talked back," my stinging and burning skin after Daddy slapped me, and my fury after hearing him lie to my mother. The image of him, the dark, ugly shape of him, came into my mind like a storm cloud.

"Do they know where you are?" Dora asked. "Did you tell anybody where you were going?"

"No," I said, in as firm a voice as I could manage. "I'll pay my way here, I promise."

David Sr. clasped his hands together, with his elbows on the table. The oilcloth covering had red and yellow flowers on it. I trained my eyes on one small section of the flower pattern and held my breath. They must not force me to go back. They must not. I was too close to the final X on my map, too close to turn around.

"I ran away," I said. "I know it sounds stupid, but I can't live with them. I hate them."

"Hate is such a strong word," Dora said softly. "Why do you feel this?"

I felt the expression on my face twisting into a grimace. I didn't know what to tell her. Could I begin to describe all the times Daddy had done things to make me cry and feel ashamed? The words were there, swirling in my head like a windstorm, but nothing came out. I thought I would choke if I tried to speak. Dora watched me for a long moment and then turned her eyes away.

"You left without telling anybody?" David Sr. asked, his hands still clasped. "Not even Edna or Bill? You walked into town?"

"Mrs. Gonzales, one of our neighbors, gave me a ride to the bus station. I had enough money for a ticket. I still have some left since it was only eight dollars to get here."

All the Wilson children, including the smallest one, four-year-old Rita, huddled close to hear me better. Their faces described their astonishment at what I was saying. None of them had ever had the slightest reason to think of running away from home.

"Did you leave a note?" David Sr. asked.

"I didn't leave a note. I suppose I could have, but I didn't. Bill is going to know where I am. He'll figure it out. I've told him—when bad things have happened before—that if something made me run away, I'd come here. He knows."

David Sr.'s face, like Bennie Shay's, told me nothing of his thoughts. I kept my eyes on his, but I couldn't read what was behind them.

"I won't go back," I said fiercely. "I'm sick of never feeling safe. You don't know how mean Daddy is. He doesn't have any friends. He bullies people and lies about everything. I won't go back, no matter what."

"You're a child yet," Dora said in her quiet voice. "You and Jake here, you're the same age, too young to make a decision like this, to leave home."

I looked at Jake. He was staring out the window at the brightening day. But I knew he was listening. I knew he was taking in every single word.

"I won't do what they want," I said, making fists with my hands. "Why should I, anyway? My parents both lie. They do what they want, never thinking about what we want."

"What lie did your father tell?" Dora asked.

I considered her question. It was not like any of the others they had asked.

"I argued with Daddy. I talked back to him. I've never done that before. I've never dared. He slapped me hard across the face," I said, my voice shaking with the memory of it. I automatically raised my hand to the cheek that had been slapped. "I was afraid he'd hit me again, as he'd done other times. But he didn't. He left me sitting there in his office and walked away. So I started to go to my room."

"On the way down the hall I heard them talking. My

mother was crying. He was telling her that I'd begged to be allowed to live with her. It was a lie. He didn't say what was really true, which is that I want to stay on the ranch, or live with Bill and Edna.

"He lied to Mother because he doesn't want me around. Before he left his office, after he hit me, he said, 'I want nothing further to do with you.' "

David Sr. dropped his eyes.

I noticed Jake's head turning slightly. Silent Jake. He would remember every word I was saying. I could tell from the way he was staring, as if he saw nothing at all while there was everything to see.

"Poor child," Dora said, her broad hand warm on my shoulder. "Poor Jamie."

I hadn't heard my name spoken since my father used it to tell me I had a smart mouth. It sounded foreign, like another person's name.

"Your father acts crazy sometimes," Linda said. "Maybe it's better you stay out here for a while."

Dora hushed her daughter. She said it was rude to call a person crazy. "Unless you know for sure" she added, with barely a smile.

"I want to stay," I said, rubbing tears away. "I won't be any trouble. I'll work and earn my way. You can give me jobs to do."

I was embarrassed. I sounded like a beggar.

A huge wave of shame came over me in that moment. I often felt shame when I talked about my parents, especially my father. My parents were not like other people's parents. They never hugged or kissed us. They said they didn't believe in raising children that way. They were cold and distant. And the air around them was cloudy with anger and tears.

My whole family was horribly different from other families. Sometimes, if I was talking to people who didn't know my family, I'd lie and pretend that they didn't fight and hurt each other. I'd make up stories about how regular and nice they were.

David Sr. took his time considering. He waited for me to get control. I pushed off the urge to weep by concentrating on the pattern of the oilcloth on the table.

"For now you stay with us, Jamie. We'll see about what to do later on," he said at last.

I took a long, deep breath. Looking at his face, I tried to smile.

He stood, flattening his palms against the oilcloth. He rubbed the surface gently with his fingers. "We'll see what to do. I need time to think about this." He went outside and shut the screen door so it wouldn't bang.

Everybody began to clear dishes and straighten up, everyone except David Jr., Jake, and the two younger boys. They went outside to join David Sr. Soon I heard the truck engine cough, roar a few times, and begin to hum.

"You rest today," Dora told me. "We'll find work for you to do soon enough."

I helped wash up. After the men and boys left, I offered Dora money for the meal. She brushed me off. I quickly realized that it was an insult to offer her money for her hospitality. She looked at me as if she felt pity and said, "You're a part of this family. There will be no exchange of money between us."

TO THE CANYON

Three days passed, then four. I felt limp and aimless, like a balloon without enough air. I was a person made of dust, not flesh and bone. I walked around with the same feeling I often had at home—that somebody was watching every move I made. I kept imagining Daddy's angry, swollen face, his heavy body lunging at me, ready to tie me in ropes and take me back.

The Wilson household had a routine, a steady and reliable beat of activity. Dora put me in charge of Rita so that I was occupied, and not completely without a reason for existing.

I hardly spoke. When someone talked to me it was about ordinary things. But I didn't feel ordinary. Every loud noise made me jump—the cicadas clattering in the trees, the cars on the dirt road, the screen door when Rita slammed it.

Nobody from my family called or showed up. This was strange. I kept thinking they must be trying to find me. It wouldn't be natural if they didn't try.

I'd been with the Wilsons for five days when David Sr. came in from work early. He smelled of horses and leather. He was a horse handler and cowhand for a rancher. In his younger days, David had kept a string of rodeo horses. He had been a rider in calf-roping and bull-riding events. He'd won prize money.

We were all seated at the supper table and eating our food when David Sr. said he was ready to pack up for the Canyon. "I got time off work," he told Dora. "We might as well get started in the morning."

The words came out in his usual way, slowly and softly, as if there wasn't anything special about what he was saying.

A shiver went through me. The Canyon was the last X on my map.

I turned to look at David Sr.'s face. I watched his eyes. He raised his fork, took a bite, and chewed. He didn't say anything more for what seemed like a very long time.

Dora was telling the others what she wanted to pack. I waited. Nobody said a word about me going. Did that mean I would go, that there wasn't any wondering to do?

"I want to go with you," I said. "The Canyon is the last X on my map."

"What map?" Linda asked, looking up from her plate.

"It's imaginary," I said. "I made it up when I left home. I saw it in my head. It's a pretend piece of white paper with an X for the bus station, an X for Window Rock, and a final X for the Canyon."

Rita's eyes lit up. "I like pretend things," she said, smiling. Dora and David Sr. both glanced at me with questions in their eyes.

A long silence followed.

"We're not going to leave you here by yourself." Dora spoke slowly, as if she weren't sure what to say.

"Nobody seems to be showing up to fetch you home," David Sr. said. He let his fork drop.

Another eternal silence.

"If they come after her, they can find her in the Canyon as well as here," David Jr. said. He was a thinner version of his father. The two of them worked together for the rancher with the horses.

"Why hasn't somebody come yet?" Linda asked, looking around the table. "You'd think they would have by now, if they were going to."

I waited to hear the words I was desperate for, that without a doubt I'd be allowed to go. People chewed. Forks and knives scraped plates. On the road in front of the house a truck made a loud noise when its driver gunned the engine.

More than once Bill had said how Navajo people don't rush things. He knew their ways from doing business with them. "They take all the time they need," he said. "They think about things before they act."

That's what's happening now, I thought. They're taking the time they need to decide what to do.

I wondered what Jake would say, if somebody asked him, about me going with them. Did he even care? Jake hardly talked to anyone, especially me. I'd known him from the first time I'd come to Chinle with Bill. Jake and I were almost exactly the same age, to the day. Our birthdays were in October. I'd seen Jake a dozen times in my life since my first visit when we were both five. Never before had he acted like I didn't exist. But he was doing that now, I thought, pretending I was invisible. It was like he could see straight through me.

Dora ended the silence. "You must go with us," she said, as if it were all of a sudden clear. "There's no better place for you."

I thought I might explode with relief.

We started to pack for the Canyon that night. Rita wanted me to help her wrap her things in her blanket. She had toys and clothes she didn't want to leave behind. She would be in the Canyon for weeks, for the rest of the summer. It was a long time for a four-year-old to go without her favorite toys.

I imagined my room at home, empty and still without me in it. I supposed it looked the way I left it. Who would change anything?

I'd brought what I needed and nothing extra—one change of clothes—a pair of jeans, clean socks, a sweater, and one jacket. I'd left the rest behind.

That night I went to use the outhouse and wash up. A barrel was set out to catch rain at the side of the house.

It wasn't the only water supply. A pump in the front yard brought clear cold water up out of the ground. The front-yard water was used for drinking and cooking; the backyard water was for cleaning up.

I unbuttoned my shirt and hung it on a nail stuck in a

post. I felt utterly alone out there. I had no worries about being seen naked. I scooped water into my hands and let it pour over my shoulders until the waist of my jeans was soaked. Brown streams of muddy water carried dust off my skin. I rubbed my stomach with my hands so hard that the muscles in my upper arms ached.

Hobos washed like this, I thought, *in rain barrels, in puddles.*

I dried off using the towel Dora had given me the first night. I put my shirt back on.

My mother would not approve of how I was living. Washing was a ritual she cherished. A person didn't wear the same shirt—much less the same underwear—two days in a row. I'd worn the same clothes for nearly a week now.

My mother's eyes were pale in her narrow face. I pictured her then, thinking of how determined she was to fuss at my sisters and me over the smallest mistakes: a bed not made, a glass of milk spilled. She never paid attention to the big things.

I whispered a prayer that nobody would show up to take me home—not that night, not ever. I wouldn't want to go with them, but I wouldn't know how to keep them from forcing me.

In the morning there was heavy work waiting for us. Two wooden-box wagons needed to be loaded. For a family so large, one wagon wasn't enough. There were two teams of skinny bay horses for pulling.

Jake was in charge of the teams. He was first up, and I could see how eager he was to get going. I offered to help with the horses.

"Not women's work," he said, looking away from me. I hated the way he wouldn't look at me. "Go help the girls. See what my mother needs."

I turned for the house, remembering how Navajo men work with the horses. Women and girls take care of the sheep and goats. So I went to help Dora.

At noon we were ready to go. The wagons were piled high with cardboard boxes of canned goods, sacks of flour and sugar, pails of honey and lard, and yarn for Dora's weaving. Dora's loom was also packed. There were endless bags of clothing. The men tossed in shovels and tools for repairing the hogan and the sheep corrals at the Canyon.

David Sr. asked Jake and the other boys to help load the seed corn. I breathed in the sweet smell of the seed. It was the same dizzying aroma that the hay fields gave off when Bill cut the alfalfa and let me ride behind him on the tractor. The seed was last to be loaded. The men grunted under the weight of the sacks. We left with David Sr. driving one team and David Jr. driving the other.

Dora sat next to her husband. The rest of us scrambled to find comfortable places in the backs of the wagons.

The wheels groaned and squeaked as the horses fought against the weight of the load. We took the main dirt road, passing through the middle of Chinle, then headed north toward the Canyon.

The town of Chinle was spread across a series of sand hills. It was thinly populated, with few cottonwood trees to offer shade. The sun-bleached look of it reminded me of home. But most people in Chinle lived in trailers that were propped up on cinderblock foundations. The trailers had plastic awnings over the windows and doors. Black rubber tires were piled on top of tin roofs to keep the roofs from blowing away.

Scattered between the trailers were government-built houses—small boxes with plywood walls and tar-paper roofs. Set back and apart from the "modern" dwellings were the hogans—low, eight-sided houses used for special occasions such as naming ceremonies and wedding feasts. Many families also had mud ovens, *hornos* we called them, behind their houses. These were used for baking the big loaves of fry bread that everyone ate.

The wind had carried tumbleweed across bare ground and between structures. Tangled bunches of the prickly, pale brown bushes were crammed under porches or trapped in doorways and at the bottoms of fence posts. Any dusty open space was strewn with weeds and trash, abandoned automobiles, and rusted farm equipment well past usefulness. Boundary lines were not clear. There were few fences except for the ones used for animal pens. Clothesline poles stood out against the sky, like guardians over front and back yards. Sheets, towels, and undershirts flapped like flags in the breeze.

There was a fair wind that noon, enough to make the fur stand up on the backs of bony dogs. These dogs, every one a mongrel, looked like strays. I knew they had owners, at least most of them did. Dogs were allowed to wander as they pleased. Nobody paid them any mind except to send them running with a yell or a kick in the ribs. Mother dogs with saggy teats on their underbellies were followed by strings of fuzzy puppies.

Flocks of chickens scattered around the wagon wheels as we passed through town. Like the dogs, they didn't seem to have owners. The wind rushed behind the fluttering chickens and forced some to lift their wings in short bursts of flight.

Both teams of horses stopped at the head of the Canyon, where the long winding trail led into it.

We saw the Canyon opening out in front of us like a wide mouth. It was smooth-sided with sandstone walls. Two channels met to form a single cut in solid rock one thousand feet deep in the earth.

The teams were whistled back into motion by the two drivers. The reins snapped and the horses noisily blew air out their nostrils.

We began rolling down the narrow trail. Jerking from side to side, the wagons shook as if they were ready to come apart. I gulped, looking down into the Canyon, trying to soak in the way sunlight and shadow danced on the rock walls.

The Canyon, the final X on my map, had that effect on people. The pure beauty of it, shimmering under the sun's glare, caused a person to gasp, to struggle for air, to wonder at the mysterious forces present there. The Navajo have an understanding about the mysteries of this place, their sacred ground.

The rift in the earth called Canyon de Chelly is sacred to the Navajo. It is so sacred that when the Navajo came back from four years of exile in Bosque Redondo in southern New Mexico, they kissed the ground and spoke to it, saying how glad they were to be home.

Jake's Fire

I perched in the back of the second wagon and stared out at the trail we were taking. I watched it vanish in clouds of white dust as I gripped the wooden frame to keep from falling. I rode high on a bundle of clothes with Rita close against me. Several of the Wilson children ran alongside the wagons when the trail allowed space for it. We took more than an hour to make the long, slow descent.

It seemed I could almost touch the space between where I was and my other life. It was that real to me, as if it had surfaces and sides. I sensed the distance expanding with every creak of the wagon wheels as they turned.

Along the Canyon bottom, there was a stream—a wide wash. When the upper trail was behind us, we rolled out onto the flats and into the cottonwoods. We came to the water's edge. The men stopped the horses and we took a breather. We wet our feet and let the animals drink from the wash.

Cottonwood forests grew thick in the bottom of the Canyon. Their shade was welcome after the wind, sun, and heat of the trail. Willows sprang up in clumps along the borders of the wash. These clumps were too dense to see through and grew straight up out of the hot sand taller than a person.

The stream was usually running, except during droughts. In the spring, the water was especially deep and thick with silt. By June and July, the runoff slowed and the stream lessened to a shallow, meandering ribbon of muddy water. The surface of the stream shimmered with reflected light that was constantly changing, depending on whether the sun or the moon was shining.

I sat by the stream and stuck my bare feet in to cool them. Some distance above me on a ledge, in a shady alcove of sandstone, was a ruin—one of many in the Canyon. These ruins were all that was left of the Anasazi people, "The Ancient Ones."

Some people say the word Anasazi means "Ancient Enemy." If you ask the Navajo, you get different answers, or maybe no answer. They keep their secrets to themselves.

The Anasazi built villages, small communities, on the rock ledges above the Canyon floor. They used stone blocks with mud for mortar. For thousands of years they lived there, raising crops of beans, squash, and corn. By now the walls of their houses had crumbled. Some ruins were no more than shapeless mounds of earth. But looking at the ruins, a person could still imagine The Ancient Ones coming and going on footpaths, growing patches of corn and beans, getting water from springs and the stream.

The Anasazi left mysterious pictures on rock walls. They hammered with stones, pecked with deer antlers, and painted with bird-feather brushes. They left behind images of mountain sheep, dancing Spirit figures, and Kokopelli, the flute player with the hunched back.

The Navajo arrived more than fifteen hundred years ago to live in the Canyon and call it their sacred ground. By then, the Anasazi had gone, to another place where they had new clan names and different lives. Today's Pueblo peoples claim the Anasazi as their ancestors.

The Navajo have since woven themselves into the landscape of the Canyon, in the same way a bird uses silk from a spider's web to make a nest stronger.

In the heat of the afternoon I sat listening to Rita and the other children shouting and splashing. I wondered how long people remembered things. Would I forget the sadness that hung so heavily in those rooms at home? Would I keep the memory of it in my head until the day I died?

I remembered every humiliation, every moment in my life when I was terrified because Daddy leveled his eyes on me. So many times I was left feeling sad—unable to forget his cruelty.

The Navajo have long memories. Their canyon places echo with their own human history. You know this from the way their places are named: Standing Cow Ruin, Canyon del Muerto (Place of the Dead), and Massacre Cave. The names of ancient pictures on walls, of old ruins and sheep camps under the trees—everything reminds the Navajo of their past. They don't want to forget. They like remembering.

Memories came into my head even when I didn't want them to. I told myself I wouldn't try to stop the flood when it started. Someday the things I wanted to remember would remain. The rest would be gone for good.

Rita ran over and shook a pair of muddy hands in my face. She was shrieking with glee. "I found it," she told me happily. "I found quicksand mud."

Canyon de Chelly was the best place we knew for quicksand mud of a certain slippery kind. It held together and slid over your fingers the way normal mud never would. It stuck to your skin and changed the color, staying in your pores for days and sometimes weeks. The mud was cool, even cold. We smeared it all over ourselves. The horses' furred muscles quivered under the layers of mud we smoothed over their rumps.

The children soon joined Rita and me at the edge of the quicksand hole. Jake was the only one who didn't come. He was sitting, like a watching crow, on a heap of canned goods and bags in one of the wagons. He was acting like he didn't care about quicksand anymore. There was no chance to call him to come play because Dora was saying it was time to go.

I crawled across bundles in the wagon to get to where Jake was sitting. The horses were starting to move. "Come on," I said. "Let's wade instead of ride."

Jake was up in a flash. He wore his black hair long and loose, down to his shoulders. It swung in front of his face so I couldn't see his eyes. The two of us were quickly over the side of the wagon and splashing in the muddy water. Jake was in the lead, with me close behind.

I watched him run. I wanted to be his friend, like before. But everything was different now—Jake had been acting so distant every time I came near.

We ran until I had to catch my breath. Jake stopped, waiting. He turned and looked back. "Come on," he said. "Don't chicken out now."

He'd teased me from the start, since I'd first met him. He would always say my name was a boy's name, and tell me that he had a secret Navajo name I wasn't allowed to know, for as long as I lived.

"Jake is my fake name," he said. "My Anglo name."

He was right. I would never have a secret name or be allowed to know his, because I wasn't Navajo.

Jake was bony and thin. He ran fast, like an antelope. I could barely keep up.

We looked for quicksand. Jake was good at spotting the wet sinkholes of mud where bubbles covered the surface like delicate lace.

I liked it that Jake knew things. He knew the Canyon trails by heart. He had them memorized. If one thing changed, if a branch of a tree fell, or if a willow tree was blown down, he'd know it. He'd spot the difference instantly.

He also loved horses the same way I did. Since the time he was eight or nine years old, he even had some of his own. It was Jake who showed me how to run alongside a horse and grab its mane to pull myself up on its back. We'd race along a stream and get soaked. Jake led on his own horse, looking back now and then to make sure I was still there and not thrown off.

Jake liked to dare me to do things. Half the time he was a regular friend—then he'd get me to do something I didn't want to, just to test me.

I saw him ahead of me, darting through the trees and splashing in the water. He was sullen when I was around him. It made me feel like everything that happened was my fault, even when I was standing still. Jake suddenly turned and raced back over the way we'd come, heading toward the wagons. I followed him. I kept waiting to see what he would do. I was afraid of making my own moves.

The wagons rolled into camp late that day, toward evening. I'd been to this same camp on earlier trips with Bill. The first thing I noticed was how everything was the way I'd pictured it. It was just the same as before.

I peered into the shadows between the cottonwood trees and saw the shadehouse. Its walls needed fixing after standing neglected all winter. Bits of blackened wood were scattered across the sandy ground—the remains of fires from another summer. Well-worn footpaths led into the woods, to the outhouse, to the stream, and to the tree where food was stored above ground so rodents wouldn't get at it.

I helped unload the wagons. Linda said, "Let the boys get the poles. They're too heavy for us." The poles were used for the hogan. Like the shadehouse, the hogan also needed fixing.

It was hard to make out the hogan, which was made with flat pine planks and roofed with brush. A thick wall of cottonwood branches hung low around it.

A pile of belongings formed on the sand. David Sr. and

Dora kept an order to the flow of belongings and supplies coming out of the wagons. Soon, with everyone helping, the work was done. Everything we'd brought had been unloaded and rested in piles under the trees.

"Help me make a supper fire," someone said.

I turned to see Jake watching me. "Come on," he said. "It's time."

I nodded and followed him. We took a narrow footpath that wound around the trees through the willow tree groves. We searched for any wood that had fallen to the earth. We looked for not-too-green branches that were old enough to burn and not just smoulder and smoke.

It was getting dark. I caught my feet on snags and roots while Jake moved swiftly, like an owl with wings instead of a human being with an armload of wood.

"Wait up," I said. "Wait for me."

For once he did. We walked back to camp in almost total darkness.

Jake told me to pick a spot for the fire. "You choose," he said, grinning.

I looked around in the gloom and picked a bare spot not far from the wagons. Soft voices drifted through the night—Dora, David Sr., and the others.

Working together, we built up a heap of twigs, with the heavier pieces of wood around the outside. Jake gave me matches in a small box that he pulled from his shirt pocket. I struck one and the fire flared right away. Its orange and yellow flames were bright and strong.

"Good," Jake said, slapping his thigh with the palm of his hand. He stood. "You build a fire like you've done it before."

"I have," I said, trying not to sound like a show-off. "We heat our rooms at home with fires in the fireplaces."

Jake didn't say anything.

The family gathered around, dragging blankets and rugs to sit on. Rita sat down directly on the sand. I reached down and touched the ground next to her. It was still warm from the heat of the day.

Within a few minutes, Rita was up and screaming. She ran around the fire, rubbing her bottom and yelling, "I got bit! Something hurt me!"

Dora grabbed her youngest girl and began to pull at layers of her clothing. "Ants," Dora said, "the red kind that bite."

"Ouch!" Linda cried. "Look! Red ants are on everything."

Sure enough, red ants were streaming out from under the spot where the fire burned. There were hundreds, maybe millions, of ants heading in every direction without order to their flight.

"You built this fire on an ant hill?" David Jr. accused his brother Jake.

"Not me. Her. It's Jamie's fire." Jake looked at me. He grinned and flipped his hair, which had fallen forward around his face, back over his shoulder.

It's Jake's fire, I thought, *not mine.*

The family got up quickly, each one scrambling to brush ants off, and moved away from the fire. Rugs and blankets were swirled up and shaken out, creating a storm of gritty sand in the air. They paid no attention to me, except for Jake, who watched my face and waited to see what I'd do—cry or be angry.

David Jr. came over and threw his blanket to one side.

He took a flaming branch out of the fire and carried it about fifteen feet away. "Come on," he said. "We'll get a new fire going."

I did what he said. I leaned into the flames and picked out a burning stick. The bangs on my forehead sizzled and smelled like burning hair. I paid no attention. I didn't care. It didn't matter to me what fried, what burned, what disappeared.

A new fire soon sent arcs of blazing light into the black spaces over our heads. Supper was ready. I was starving. We ate a meal of fried potatoes, chunks of bread, and bacon that had been cooked until the fat pooled and bubbled in the frying pan.

I wondered if Jake planned every single thing he did in order to humiliate a person. But how could he? I was the one who had picked the place for the fire. Jake knew every-thing about this spot in the camp where he'd been coming all his life. He knew where the ant hill was all along. He might have told me, but he didn't.

The moon was high, almost full, when it was time to sleep. I thought about home and wondered who might be looking for me.

I slept with Rita next to me. One of the boys loaned me a sleeping bag and I shared it with Rita, along with her blanket, which she rarely let go of.

I asked the boy about his sleeping bag, "Don't you need it yourself?"

"No," he said. "I'd rather sleep in the wagon bed. Too many ants crawling around in the dark."

A CONVERSATION

For two days we worked on the shadehouse, where Dora wanted her loom set up. We replaced rotted poles with new ones. Fresh cottonwood boughs were gathered for roof thatch.

Linda took me along when she went to bring the Wilson sheep, a flock of thirty-five animals, back to camp. The flock had been joined with another family's flock of sheep during the winter and spring. It was a six-mile walk, round trip, and coming back was slow. The sheep moved lazily. They were more eager to nibble grass than keep up a steady pace.

David Sr. spent half a day making sure the corral had no holes in it that were big enough for a lamb to squeeze through.

Dora took a pair of scissors and cut my shirt. She trimmed off the sleeves and stitched a hem so my arms were bare. "Next time we go to Chinle we'll visit the thrift store," she said. "We can get you some clothes." As she spoke, she ran her hand through my hair. "And maybe a ribbon for your hair," she added.

Early in the afternoon of the second day in camp I followed Jake as he climbed the front of a cliff. We were friends again, although we hardly spoke. The rocks were smooth and warm under our hands.

Jake knew where the hand and foot holes were in the slippery sandstone. The holes had been worn centuries before by people climbing in that same place. We got high enough to look down and see magpies flying over the tops of cottonwood trees, their tail feathers flickering in the sunlight.

On the way back down the wall he said, "Your people are coming for you."

"How do you know?"

"I just know."

I tried to shrug off his certainty, but a knot began to tighten in my stomach.

We walked back into camp, and I saw Dora talking to a tall Navajo man I didn't recognize. He'd come into the Canyon with a wagon and team. The reins of his horses were looped around a cottonwood tree next to the shadehouse.

"Here she is," Dora said. "Come here, Jamie."

I went to her. She rested her arm on my shoulder.

"Your parents are in Chinle, at the motel," Dora told me. "They want you to come there. Joe has been sent to get you."

I heard Jake's words again. How had he known?

Joe smiled at me and said, "Hello."

"Hello," I said, keeping my eyes on his belt. It was a dark leather strap with fifty-cent pieces sewn to it. "I don't want to go," I said quietly to Dora. "I don't have to go with him, do I?"

"Yes," she said flatly. "You do."

A coldness fell over me, a weariness. I had no energy, even to focus my eyes or breathe. I felt like a leaf that had broken off a stem and was sliding down through the air to the ground.

Dora said nothing more. No one said anything. They all stood in silence, staring.

I got into the wagon and took a seat on the rough plank where the driver sat. Joe climbed in and sat next to me. We began to roll, and Dora moved close to the wagon. She said, "Tell them you can stay with us. Tell them that."

Dora stepped back and turned. I watched her walk away, her skirt swirling around her legs. Would I ever see her again?

I didn't know who was waiting for me in Chinle. What did Dora mean by "my parents"? My father and the woman he would be marrying—or my mother and her future husband? I tried to picture who would be there as the wagon rumbled alongside the stream and up the narrow winding trail to town.

My mother stood on the motel porch, her hands gripping each other as if they were having a private battle. I could see she had been crying. Her pale eyes were wet. The skin around them was red and puffy. Behind her stood John, the man who was going to be my stepfather.

John was a slight person, except for a thickness to his neck and his round, red-spotted cheeks. He avoided my gaze. Instead, he looked past me at Joe, who waited in the wagon, the reins loose in his fingers. "What are you waiting for?" John seemed to be asking Joe, but no words came out.

"Oh, my dear child," my mother exclaimed. "Oh, dear. Bill was right. He said you'd be out here. What a place to come to. Are you mad? Have you lost your senses?"

She said words like *mad* and *crazy* and *lost your senses* when she didn't understand something.

"Come here. Let me give you a hug."

I went to her. She smelled of soap and dust. The feel of her palms on my arms was damp. I didn't want to touch her, but when she hugged me, I let her.

"You're coming back with us today," she said. "Immediately. It's best for all concerned. We'll forget about this running away business. We'll simply put it behind us and not speak of it again."

It sounded strange. Was it humanly possible to put something like running away from home behind you, and to never speak of it again?

I wanted to tell her that people run away for reasons. Didn't she know what mine were? I was terrified of Daddy. She never did anything to save me when he was around. She had no idea what it was like when she and Daddy were away. It was so peaceful. We never had to worry.

I was thinking the words but not saying them. Mother knew I wasn't listening to her. Then she did something that she often did when she wanted one of her children to pay attention, when she wasn't being heard. She came close to me and, with one hand, lifted up my chin with her thumb and forefinger. I hated that gesture.

I wrenched myself away. She spoke to my back. I could hear the tears welling in her voice. "Why do you have to be so difficult?"

I turned around and said, "I just can't go back with you, that's all. I can't."

John took my mother's arms from behind. He stared at me and said, "You're going to do what your mother wishes. For once you're going to obey her."

"It's all right, John," my mother said, composing herself. "Let me handle this. Wait for us in the room. We'll be along in a minute."

I could not imagine anything more lonely and sad than to be in the same motel room with John and my mother. The idea of this, all at once vivid in my mind, separated me from her even more.

My mother had always told me I was "the difficult child." To her it was odd that I liked to be alone, hike in the hills, and ride my horse. She hated my friends. "They are not like us," she'd say. "Why don't you pick nice girls to play with, your own kind?"

Seeing her on the motel porch, with John's white face behind her, deepened my certainty of the space between us. Our separateness was invisible, yet real enough to touch.

John did not go to the room. He walked to the far end of the motel porch and lit a cigarette. He kept his back to us as blue-gray circles of smoke rose over his head.

"Now look, dear, you must come home. The Wilsons

don't want you. We know this. To begin with, they can't afford to keep you, with all the children they have."

She might have been describing sheep, not children.

"They do want me," I said softly. "Dora told me to tell you. I can stay with them. She said it's okay. They don't mind."

My mother's hands twisted and turned, wringing each other. This was a sign that she was confused and bewildered.

"You can't stay here, because this is not your home," she said. Her tone was distant now, and her voice was even, without emotion. "You have a perfectly good home, and you know it. Your father and I have provided very nicely for you and your sisters and your brother. Changes happen in our lives, and we must learn to live with them."

"I don't have a home," I said.

"I am at a loss," my mother said, rubbing her palms together. I knew she hated the heat and dust. The heat gave her terrible headaches. She was starting to withdraw from our struggle, our clash of wills, but she wasn't ready to admit it yet.

"I don't know what to do. Your father won't take you. You say you won't live with John and me. I simply don't know what to do. You're a child, Jamie. How can you be so impossibly stubborn?"

"I want to be someplace where it's peaceful. It's peaceful here. Bill and Edna said they would let me visit them, once they get settled in their new place in Texas."

"You are such a child," she said, looking at me as if for the first time ever. "Such a child."

"I'm old enough to know what I want, where I want to be."

"I've never known what to do with you," my mother said.

"I have to be honest and say it. You're nothing like your sisters or your brother."

I stood there, watching her, listening, and wondering how she could miss seeing the truth of everything.

Another silence came between us, a sharp and hard one. I pictured my twin sisters, two years older than I, who were locked together in wordless agreement with each other. And the boy, small and thin with soft brown eyes and blond hair, who was my brother. But I hardly knew him. He was so frequently wrapped in my mother's arms. He stared out from the safety of her lap with a small face that expressed only wonder and doubt.

Joe's horses snorted and stamped their feet. They were impatient to be moving again. I knew my mother wanted our conversation to be over. I knew in her heart she didn't care if I stayed. I could read her thoughts. It would be better for her, with John in her life, to have one less child to think about.

How could I convince her she must leave me here? I searched my mind for the words. None came.

I heard the breath entering and leaving my mother's body. I heard her sigh.

Finally, she spoke and said, "Clearly you cannot stay here for long. However, it might be best for now. It's probably fine to have you settled somewhere, even in this God-forsaken wilderness, while we get the ranch business worked out. Yes, I think it's best. As usual it will be up to me to explain everything to your father."

She never explained anything or made decisions, even minor ones, about our family. She was making a decision now, and I could see how much she hated it. Relief was swelling inside me, as if the sun were getting brighter in the sky.

"Thanks, Mother," I whispered. "I'll be fine, I promise."

I had always known to be careful with her, because she was fragile, easily hurt.

"I'm going now," I said, reaching up as if to tap her shoulder. "Joe's waiting."

"I only paid him to bring you here, not to take you back," she said, confused again. "He'll want more money."

She moved down the length of the porch to where John was standing. He still had his back to us. She grabbed for his arm with a sudden, awkward gesture. For a small moment they embraced. John looked over my mother's shoulder at me. His face was a mask. I hoped desperately that he wouldn't try to change her mind.

My mother gave Joe money to take me back into the Canyon, to the Wilsons' camp. "And take this," she said, giving him an extra twenty dollars. "She'll need to get some clothes. It would be so helpful if you could take her. That way I won't have to send things out. In any case, I wouldn't be sure how to do that."

Joe folded the twenty and stuck it into his shirt pocket.

"Don't worry, Mother." I spoke before Joe had a chance to.

"Of course I am going to worry," my mother said with exasperation. She brushed her fine hair away from her face, tucking wisps of it behind her ears. "I have every reason to worry. You must at least have what you need to wear." It was like her to be concerned about my wardrobe, as if it somehow mattered.

I got back into the wagon. I didn't know what to say to her. Joe kept his eyes off my face. I didn't have to find words for him. He wasn't expecting or asking for any.

Joe urged the team of horses into motion, speaking softly in his own language.

"Well dear, good-bye," my mother said. "Perhaps I'll send Bill out here, before he leaves for Texas, to see how you are. We'll have to get you back somehow, but we'll cope with that later. I want you to promise you'll be fine. You'll behave yourself? You'll make yourself useful to poor Dora?"

"Promise," I said, giving her a weak wave and resenting the way she used the word *poor* to describe Dora.

Once we were moving, I asked Joe not to stop. "Dora told me she'd take me to the thrift store later," I explained, "so we don't have to stop."

Joe nodded. It was fine by him. "I'll give Dora the money," he said.

I thought it would be dangerous to stop the wagon and break the spell of what was happening. There might still be a way my mother and John could force me to go back with them. I couldn't stand to take that chance, no matter what.

THE RACE

I climbed down from Joe's wagon half a mile short of the Wilson camp. Joe's own camp was in a different direction. It would save time for him to let me off there, at a place where two trails met. He gave me a smile and a nod and said, "Good luck."

He'd hardly spoken the whole time. I could see he was shy, but it's not in the nature of Navajo people to go looking into other people's business anyway.

"Thanks," I said, waving. He rolled off as the wagon wheels slipped and slid on white river stones that were half hidden in the sand. What must he think, seeing a white girl left to live with a Navajo family in a sheep camp? The conversation between me and my mother made me feel ashamed, and I knew Joe had heard most of it. I wished I could know what he thought.

At the edge of the stream I stopped. I waded in a few feet and stared at my reflection in the water. A lonely ache was stuck inside me. I'd gotten my way. Somehow I had convinced Mother to let me stay in the Canyon. But it was a terrible win. It proved they didn't care.

I must look different, I thought, but the face I saw staring back at me was the same as before—the same one I saw in the bus window.

I walked on and came to a bend, a place where the water, the color of chocolate milk, rippled as it turned. It looked thick, with small lumps traveling down the middle. I waded out further and stopped to let the current carry sand out from under the bottoms of my feet. The water was only slightly cooler than bath water.

Just beyond the bend I saw Rita. She stood on the bank holding a handmade willow fishing rod. Her line was a piece of string that floated loosely on the top of the water, refusing to sink.

"Rita," I called out. "Having any luck?"

"Not yet," she said, throwing me a glance before returning her dark-eyed gaze to the end of her line. "Where've you been? You were gone a long time."

"Town."

"How'd you get to town? I didn't see you go. How come I didn't get to go with you?"

"I went to see someone, a person you don't know."

"Who? You could have at least taken me. I wouldn't have been any trouble."

"My mother. I went to see my mother."

Rita shot me another look, her eyes round and wide, that expressed her surprise. "Does she want you back? Are you going to leave and go with her?"

"I'm staying," I said, kicking at the water with my feet, making showers of yellowish brown drops. "I get to stay."

"You're scaring the fish, doing that," Rita said, her eyes focused on my legs. "I'm glad you get to stay. You're my friend by now. I want you to stay with us and not leave."

I smiled, watching the little girl. She was convinced she'd catch a fish out of the stream. The water was so muddy you couldn't see your own foot six inches under water. She had no proper line or hook, but still she meant to catch something.

I thought of my little brother. He was three, a year younger than Rita. To me, watching her, he seemed a million light years younger. "If it's all the same to you, I'll watch you fish for a while," I said.

"It's okay, I don't mind," Rita said. "But you can't talk or splash. It scares the fish if you make noise."

I sat on the sand and studied the girl's face. It was filthy, with a runny nose, smears of dirt, and black streaks of ash from the cooking fire. Her chest was bare. She wore red cotton shorts, faded with age, that were hand-me-downs from her sisters. Her skin was a smooth brownish color, like juniper berries, or like deer skin when it's been tanned.

I envied her.

Rita was not like most Navajo children I'd met, especially not like the girls. She was talkative and stubborn. Often she was not where she was supposed to be, which caused her mother to worry.

Rita knew what she wanted when it came to playing and having fun. She was opinionated about everything and spoke up even when she wasn't asked to. When she misbehaved and heard words of gentle warning from her mother, sisters, brothers, or father, she was respectful. She listened, but you could see the flash of determination in her eyes, a flash that said she would, in the end, have her own way.

I'd shared a sleeping place with Rita from my first night with the Wilsons—at first in her bed in the Chinle house, and now on the ground in camp with a cotton bedroll for a mattress. Rita was rarely still, even in sleep. She thrashed and squirmed all night, so real were her dreams. In the mornings, when I told her how much she'd moved and talked in her sleep, she'd say, "I was an antelope last night" or "I was an eagle and I flew across the desert to the mountains."

Rita was free. That's what I envied. She was treated like a whole person, not less than one because she was four, or because she was a girl, or acted silly at times. She was never humiliated.

I liked Rita's defiance. She was a bright and shiny creature, like a brilliant cactus flower in a dry and dusty place. I wished I knew what it felt like to belong somewhere the way she did, to a clan that would never betray her.

It was getting late. The light in the Canyon shifted and changed every second, the shadows stretching and bending, the sunlight splashing on walls, inching forward, vanishing and returning. It was a slow dance of color in constant motion.

Insects buzzed in the trees—cicadas rubbing their back legs together. The noises tumbled in the air. They spread and fell around our ears.

Ravens landed on the sand, pecked, bounced a few times, and were gone.

I lay on my back and closed my eyes. I told myself the sadness would pass away. Someday I would struggle to remember ever having it. That's how it would be. I'd feel safe everywhere I went. I wanted to believe that. I had escaped, and they were letting me stay where I wanted to be. I was lucky.

Rita's damp, sticky hand touched my face. I sat up, startled.

"Didn't mean to scare you," she said, bringing her face so close to mine our noses touched. She held my face between her two sticky hands. "Were you sleeping?"

"Just thinking."

"What about? I want to know. Friends share secrets—didn't you know that? You have to tell me because I'm your friend."

"I was thinking about you. How good you are at fishing."

"I'm not good," she insisted, pulling away. She stood, looking at me, her hands on her hips. "I didn't catch one single fish."

"That's okay," I said. "Maybe they're not biting because they're full. Come on, let's go. The fish aren't hungry. It's time we were back, anyhow. Dora will be wondering."

Dora was not in camp when we got there. Jake and his brother Manuel, who was nine, were sitting by the shade-house whittling with their pocket knives. Each one held a small stub of cottonwood in his fingers. I couldn't tell what sort of sculptures they had in mind to make.

"Are you staying?" Jake asked. He didn't look up. He kept his eyes on his work.

"Yes."

"Good," he said. "I'm glad."

"Everybody's glad," Rita shouted into her brother's ear. "Especially me."

When Dora got back, she came to where I stood and put her hand across my shoulder. I wasn't shorter than her by much, just a few inches. She looked at me without saying anything.

"I can stay," I said. "My mother says it's okay. Joe has twenty dollars for you, for buying me clothes. He'll give it to you sometime."

Dora smiled. "Very good," she said. "I am relieved. Now, it's time to help with supper. Where is everybody? We're having visitors tonight."

No sooner had she spoken than we heard the rumbling and clanking of an approaching wagon. A few minutes later the wagon came into view, pulled by a pair of dark roan horses with black manes and tails. The wagon bed was filled with grandmothers and grandfathers and uncles and cousins.

Joe rode in, this time on his horse, without the wagon. He talked to Dora privately, and I watched as he gave her the money. Then he joined the rest of us. I wondered what he'd told her, how much of what he'd seen and heard.

Rita, delighted to see her relatives, ran from one to another. She wrapped her arms around their legs, then flew off, squealing with happiness. She loved lots of company.

We ate under the trees. The air filled with the rhythms of

74

voices. Much of the talk was about which families were in the Canyon that summer, and which were not.

It puzzled me how news traveled in that place without telephones. People lived miles from each other, but news always got around, and quickly, too.

The relatives admired the children, how this one or that one had grown, how beautiful was one child's hair, or another's eyes. One of Rita's uncles whispered to her that she had eyes as dark and shiny as a water beetle's back.

Laughter and stories went on into the night. A coyote howled once, an owl hooted. The supper fire burned down to a ring of embers that glowed like dragon eyes.

I slept without waking in the night, not bothered for once by Rita's squirms. At sunrise, Jake woke me by whispering in my ear.

"Come on," he said. "Wake up. We're going to find the horses."

I trailed after Jake, Linda, and Manuel, who was called Lito, with Rita's hand tightly wrapped in mine. She wanted to come along and not be left behind. At first, Jake had said she couldn't come.

"She's too small," Jake said.

"I'll watch her," I told him.

Horses roamed free in the Canyon. I wondered how Jake and the others knew which way to look for them.

"There's a sweetgrass meadow up in Canyon del Muerto," Linda told me. "That's where they are."

We walked for an hour. For the last part, Rita rode piggyback, her tangled head of hair resting on my shoulder.

"Told you she's too small," Jake said.

I ignored him. I liked carrying Rita.

"Look," Jake said, beginning to run. "There they are."

Five horses stood in a meadow, the pale green grass lit by morning light. There were three roans, one bay, and a pinto.

The horses turned their heads and eyed us as we approached, attentive to our movements. They had run free for so long. I could see they were skittish and wary.

The pinto began to pitch, then lope, circling the others, kicking up dust and shaking its head.

"My horses," Jake said, laughing. "Pretty, aren't they?"

They were more than pretty. They were beautiful.

Rita slid to the ground and started running, and soon we were all running, like Jake, toward the horses. In minutes, Lito and Jake each had a horse by the mane. Linda was chasing a strawberry roan. Rita, her eyes wide, kept out of harm's way by racing along the edge of the meadow with her arms in the air.

"Ride this one, Jamie," Jake shouted, coming near. "Quick! Jump on." It was the pinto he gave me.

We rode all that day, two on a horse or solo, Rita always with me.

We splashed through the stream, making deep tracks in the mud. The horses were pumped up with energy, with a desire to run and to stretch their legs.

When the horses were tired and unwilling to run any longer, we slowed to a walk and explored side canyons. We went single file because the canyons were so narrow. The hooves of the horses clanged like bells against the hardness of the rocks. We shouted back and forth to each other as we reached with our arms because if you stretched you could touch both walls at once. Our voices left our throats, bounced off sandstone, and rang back as echoes in our ears.

The next morning, after a breakfast of black coffee, bacon, and fry bread, I asked Jake if we could ride his horses again. He said yes.

That day and the one after were much the same. Work was done in the mornings, families were visited, meals were prepared and eaten. We found time to ride in the afternoons and evenings.

The hours were marked by day and night, by the sun in the sky or the sun going down and the moon rising. The sadness was burning away, leaving me the way smoke drifts into thin air.

Then I met Michelle.

One afternoon when I was riding with Lito and Jake, we turned a corner and Michelle was standing there in front of us.

She lived with her family in a camp not far from the Wilsons'. She was close to my age, with short cropped hair and the slightest start of breasts under her T-shirt.

"Hello," Jake said, his voice sullen.

"Hello to you," Michelle said. She sounded sarcastic. "How long have you been down here?" she asked, eyeing Jake. "How long?"

"Don't know, exactly," Jake answered. "I can't remember. A while."

"Who is this?" Michelle asked, pointing at me with one finger, keeping her eyes on Jake. "A friend of yours?"

"Yeah," Jake answered. "She's a friend. Her name is Jamie."

"Where's she from? She staying with you?"

"Yeah," Jake answered slowly. "She is."

"How come?" Michelle wanted to know. "How come a white girl is staying with you?"

"Because we asked her to, that's why," Lito said, angrily.

"Oh," Michelle dropped her voice. "Can she ride? Does she race?"

I wondered why she didn't ask me directly, straight out.

"She rides good," Lito said. "She races, too."

I was invisible. They were having a conversation about me as if I weren't there.

"Then let's have a race," Michelle said. She turned to look at me. "I like races."

She came over and reached for one of my feet. She gripped my ankle in her hand and stared into my eyes. "You, white girl, will you race with me?"

"I don't know, I guess so. If you want."

I didn't know what to say to her. I could see she was full of hatred for me, but she didn't even know me. How could she hate somebody she didn't know? It made me mad the way she held my ankle. I wanted to jerk my leg away, but I was afraid of what she'd do.

"When? Tomorrow too soon for you? How about tomorrow?"

"In the morning," Jake said. "By the meadow."

I looked at Jake. His eyes were narrowed like a coyote's eyes. He stared at Michelle full in the face.

"Okay then," Michelle said, letting go of my leg. She tossed her head. I watched her walk a few yards, striding in a way that showed how little she thought of the rest of the world, especially of Lito, Jake, and me. It was almost funny, her defiant stroll across the sand, except that it wasn't.

We turned and rode off. I looked twice over my shoulder, only to see Michelle staring after us. She looked smaller and more unimportant, the further away we got.

"She's evil," Lito said, half under his breath.

"She's just crazy," Jake said, laughing. "She's wrong in the head."

"How can she be crazy?" I asked. "She's only a kid."

I needed to ask questions, to know about her. Everything had happened so fast back there at the place where we'd met. A horse race between that strange girl and me was about to happen. I wasn't ready.

"She hates whites," Lito said. "She was sent to boarding school in Window Rock because she was being bad, doing dumb stuff. She lives with her grandparents. They thought she'd get better if they sent her away. She only got worse. Now she won't even go to school. Being in that school made her hate whites even more."

"No matter what you do she'll hate you," Jake said. "She'll hate you because of your skin. Even if you give her snuff she'll be mean to you."

"Snuff? You mean chewing tobacco?" I knew what snuff was. I'd seen cowboys on the ranch with tins of the brown stringy stuff that made your teeth black if you used it regularly.

"Yeah. She's addicted to it. Her uncles bring it to her from Gallup. Her uncles are bad Indians," Jake said, laughing again.

"You'll be good tomorrow," Lito said, looking for a chance to reassure me. "You'll see. You ride good—better than her any day."

I looked down along the body of the horse I was riding, the pinto. His legs were long and slender. He was small by some standards, as if he had mustang in him, but he was powerful. He was thick in his chest, and he loved to run. There was no doubt of that in my mind.

I had to accept the challenge of the race. That was obvious. Jake and Lito would think I was a big baby if I turned it down. Besides, I could trust them. If they thought I could win, maybe I could.

I'd raced at home, plenty of times, with Bill and with the Hispanic kids who lived near us. These races, on a half-mile stretch of dirt road north of the ranch, were fast and sometimes dangerous. I'd won those home races a few times.

That night I had dreams, bad dreams I couldn't remember in the morning. I felt jittery eating breakfast, doubting there could even be a race. I wanted to walk quietly away and forget the whole thing. Michelle's face, taunting, old-looking for her age, came into my mind. I had no choice but to be there. I had to be willing to ride the pinto Jake had given me, saying the horse was mine for as long as I was in the Canyon.

When the sun came over the Canyon rim, the height of the walls was revealed gradually and slowly in the rising light. Stones glowed with a red color, like the color of blood. The Canyon bottom was green, gold, and shiny by seven-thirty. It was time to go and meet Michelle.

The air was fresh and still cool as we rode up the Canyon. The day quivered with excitement, as if it were ready for anything. The only sounds were bird songs, the breathing of the horses, and the noises of horse hooves on stones and hard ground.

I was determined to act brave. Bill's advice would be, "Don't show her you're afraid, even if you are."

At the meadow, Jake caught the pinto and brought him over to me. Jake's face was wearing an amused expression mixed with flashes of the boldness I often saw in his eyes. The race was Jake's challenge to me, as well as one from Michelle.

Lito was serious and frowning, and he looked worried.

"Watch out for her tricks," the younger boy said. "She's an outlaw."

Michelle appeared, riding bareback on a large black horse with two white socks on its front legs. Like the rest of us, Michele rode with no bridle or halter. She gripped the mane of the horse with one hand and waved the other in the air. Her feet flew up from the sides of the horse when she called out. She screamed like the eagles I'd heard in the hills.

Jake drew a line in the sand with a willow stick. "Here," he said. "This is the start. Down there where the wall curves, that's the finish. It's a quarter-mile race."

"I'll count to three, and then you go," Jake said.

Michelle brought her horse close to mine. Our legs touched and brushed against each other. She grinned, showing teeth that were uneven but perfectly white.

I could smell the heat and sweat coming off her horse. She had run him up the Canyon, I could tell. She had winded him. The pinto was still fresh.

We sat in complete silence for a long moment, making ourselves ready in our minds, the way people do before a fight. Michelle turned her face away and, from the corner of my eye, I saw her peer through her horse's ears, as if she were trying to see something too far away to focus on.

Jake started counting.

Jake had trained the pinto himself, mostly for speed. The animal leapt away from the start like an arrow shot from a bow. I could hear his deep gasps as he worked to bring extra air into his lungs.

I summoned all the courage I had. I knew I didn't want to let Bill down by losing this race.

Michelle rode alongside me with her arms high, her elbows at the same level as her ears, her heels beating against the sides of her horse.

The two horses hung close, nose to nose, neither one in the lead. Dust flew up—a choking, fine white powder. I kicked harder, leaning forward across the horse's neck, urging for all I was worth.

Then, suddenly, Michelle yanked on her horse's mane, throwing him into a swerve that forced his head in front of the pinto's nose. My horse was thrown off stride. I leaned to the left to balance my weight so I could keep from falling. The radiance of the morning sun struck me in the eyes. I was blinded by looking directly into the sun.

My horse got his rhythm going again, but not soon enough. Michelle crossed the finish line half a horse length ahead of me.

We both pulled up, breathing hard. The horses blew shots of wetness out their nostrils. Their sides heaved from their effort. Bubbles of yellowish foam dripped from their mouths.

"So, white girl, you lose." Michelle jeered, her voice harsh and scratchy. "You lose and I win, just the way I figured."

Lito and Jake ran up, their faces twisted with rage. Jake's long hair flew around his head like a swarm of bees.

"You cheated," Lito yelled. "You didn't win fair because you cheated, the same way you always do."

"What do you mean, the way I always do? What do you know about anything?" Michelle threw a black look at us before she turned her horse and headed down the Canyon. "Your white girl is the loser this time," she yelled over her shoulder.

We watched her go. No one said anything. The black horse churned up clumps of mud crossing the stream bed. Michelle had her tired horse running, even now, after the race was over.

"Lunatic! Cheater! Bully! Witch!" The words exploded out of Lito's mouth.

"Be careful calling people witches," Jake warned.

"She *is* one," Lito said with conviction.

"I was sure you'd win," Jake said to me. For a moment he sounded just like his father, David Sr., his voice soft and hard to hear. "You'd have won if she hadn't cheated." He stamped the earth with the heel of his foot. "Maybe Lito is right. Maybe she is a witch."

"There's no such thing," I said, almost whispering. "They're imaginary, from stories, not real."

"You're wrong," Jake said. He looked at me sideways, hesitating to say more. "Witches exist. They're people with a sickness inside. They do harm on purpose. Witches are powerful. They don't feel bad after hurting someone. They're dangerous."

"Like my father," I said, this time in a whisper. "Just like him."

"What?" As Lito turned to look at me, the sun was in his eyes. He shaded them with his hand. "What did you say?"

"Nothing."

I watched as Jake dropped back into being sullen. He hated it that I'd lost. It was all over his face, even in the way that he stood. He kept his eyes off mine, which was a clear sign of what he was thinking.

If only I'd turned the pinto sooner, or if I'd been faster to begin with, or if he'd been riding instead of me. . . . I would have cried, except the two of them were there, watching me.

I closed my eyes and slid down off the pinto to the ground. I felt listless and weary. My body felt like it weighed a thousand pounds.

Jake came to take the pinto. He slipped his slender brown fingers through the fineness of the mane hair and rubbed the horse's wet nose. He smoothed the dampness on the animal's neck. He spoke words to the horse in a voice too low for me to hear. He came over and stood next to me, bending his head so his eyes were on the sand.

"Watch out for her," he said. "She's your enemy now."

LEAF SANDALS

Jake had not found fault with me outright, but the expression on his face—the way he stood there wordless after his warning about Michelle—told me what was in his mind.

Warmth grew out of the sand under my bare feet, tendrils of it like thick vines. I felt a rush of the old familiar sadness, a dark wind swelling in my chest. That's where the sadness lived, inside my chest.

I didn't know what to do.

Lito and Jake were stiff like marble statues. The pinto's nose rested comfortably in Jake's palms.

Lito flopped down on the sand. That's when I decided to leave them, to walk away by myself.

The day was new but it felt over. The sun threw down a roaring heat that poured into my bones. There were no clouds in the sky.

I didn't belong there. I didn't belong anywhere. I was a vagrant, a fugitive, a stray. I was a mongrel, like the dogs wandering around Chinle.

I moved the way I imagined a prisoner does, slumped over with my head down and without a destination.

I came to a well-used trail that ran up to the rim of the Canyon. I followed it. I looked behind me to see space opening and widening under the sky as I climbed. The creases and ripples of wave marks had been etched into the rock over endless time. It was as if water had washed against the walls, wearing away the sandstone. There was no water now, just heat and dust. The patterns looked like the ridges in dunes that are shaped by sand blowing in the wind.

The world was frozen in time. It was so quiet that morning. Everything living seemed to have died, to have left and gone elsewhere.

The rocks were the color of antelope hide or owl feathers. Everything seemed colored that way, with a sunlit paleness. Nothing moved but light and shadow, rays splashing brightness.

At the top, more than a mile from the bottom, I stood and looked in all four directions. The Navajo have colors for each direction. West is yellow for twilight, east is white for dawn, south is blue for daylight, and north is black for night.

I would go north. I knew it didn't matter where I went, but north felt right. I would be a nomad, a hobo.

The thought made me shiver while beads of sweat

dampened my skin. I wouldn't have to know directions or where I was going. All I needed to do was go, and keep on going, until my journey was over.

As I started off, a pair of ravens careened out of the sky. They were the first birds I'd noticed that morning. They came from behind me and flashed into view. The sun reflected off their black feathers. They dove as if a collision with the earth had to happen. They swept up at the last second, their dark bodies rolling as they climbed, their broad wings spread wide. They played in the air, showing off. I watched them disappear.

When they were gone, I dropped my eyes to the ground. Insect tracks spread every which way, like footprints. Zig-zag lines crossed and criss-crossed each other.

I followed one of the trails, although it was barely visible for how delicate it was. After some searching, and losing the trail once before finding it again, I discovered a milli-pede had made the marks.

The millipede was three inches long, the dark wine color of dried blood. It was wrapped in a tight embrace with a legless creature that had a black back and a red-and-yellow belly.

The two might have been mating, but the truth was that the millipede was being eaten alive. It was a horrible sight. I saw no sign of a struggle, just the two animals hugging. I crawled closer to watch.

It made me think of my father. Daddy killed things sud-denly, without a need or a reason. A terror that you could see in his eyes came over him. Once he killed a bull snake by the ditch. The snake had been trying to get away. He beat it to death with a shovel and then chopped it into bits. A lot of snakes had come out that summer. They showed themselves in the plain light of day because there was a drought. The rains had missed us, and thirst made snakes and other animals desperate.

Bill had figured out how the snake had died. He said to Edna, and I overheard, "There was no cause for that snake to be killed. A bull snake is best kept around a place. Eats prairie dogs and mice. That was a grandfather snake, too." Bill talked about that snake for a long time, always under his breath, and never where Daddy could hear.

Daddy was terrified of spiders, insects, and snakes. He smashed and destroyed any that crossed his path. His loathing of these animals made me determined to search them out. The smallest creatures, always reliable in their comings and goings, gave me comfort. Knowing the simple details of their lives somehow made me feel better about my own.

I'd especially loved horned lizards. They seem like baby dinosaurs, with prickly skins and horns over their eyes. I looked around, searching for places where horned lizards might be hiding in the sandy soil, which was their way of finding relief from the heat. They buried their bodies in the sand, all but their heads and noses.

Ants crawled everywhere on the soil. Horned lizards eat ants. The ants made me think I would see lizards.

There were no lizards, and nothing to hear but a faint humming. Was it made by insects or by the earth spinning? I couldn't tell where the hum came from. After a while I got up and moved on.

The buzz of a rattlesnake stopped me. I'd been taught to freeze when I heard that buzz, and to locate the snake before taking another step.

I soon saw where the snake was hiding, under a sagebrush ten feet away. Its scales were the colors of the bush above it—a greenish gray-brown, with black stripes and flashes of white.

It was beautiful, with a lizardlike head. And it was dangerous. What if it struck me? There'd be no chance of getting help.

I wondered why I didn't feel scared, like I ought to have done.

According to Bill, rattlesnakes don't strike unless they are forced to. You practically have to stand on top of one, or brush against its face with your foot.

They could "hear" you coming, by sensing your walking vibrations, and they would slither out of sight. I wondered why this one had not disappeared when I approached.

Maybe the snake felt safe, even with me there. I stayed and watched the snake. It stopped buzzing. The flicking tongue, and the stare from its eyes that seemed sightless, cast a spell over me. The eyes were tucked deep under bony ridges.

The snake curved its body into a graceful arc barely inches above the ground, like a rope uncoiling in slow motion. The reptile blended completely with the soil, the sage around it, even the air, as it slithered away. After it was gone I wondered if I'd ever really seen it. Maybe I was imagining it.

The scream of a hawk's cry traveled down the sky. I

shut my eyes and imagined that the sound was water spilling down from a high place in fat, shiny droplets landing on my head.

The inside of my mouth had no wetness to it. My tongue was dry and sore.

Looking up and shading my eyes with my hands, I saw two red-tailed hawks soaring over my head. Their acrobatics in flight told me they were a mated pair. Their calls were a warning to the world that an enemy was coming into their territory.

The hawks looped and swung. The sun was bright on their stomach feathers, throats, and underwings. Had there been a way, I would have turned myself into a hawk and joined them in the air.

Sand rivers ran hot under my feet, intense and burning. I pictured the sun's fire swallowing me in its fury, turning me to ashes. My remains would end up blown away in the wind. There wouldn't be the least trace left behind.

Beetle footprints were maps on the sand, maps of beetle journeys. I found solace in trying to imagine the lives of the tiniest desert animals.

I found the claw marks and tail drags of rodents, and the long footprint of a kangaroo rat. Animals had passed so many times over a game trail that a rut had formed.

I came upon a coyote den and thought about squeezing through the opening into the chamber underground. But I was too big to fit. I could tell from the spider webs strung across the opening that no coyote had been there in a while. Silky strands hung limp, with dust and bits of leaf clinging to them. I couldn't find the spiders that had made the webs.

They were there somewhere, but they were hiding.

The sun reached the top of the sky. My feet hurt so much from the heat of the sand that I couldn't stand it any more. I sat down in the shade of a yucca to look at the bottoms. Blisters the size of fifty-cent pieces had formed and broken open. The soles of my feet were raw and, in a few spots, red with bleeding.

I held my feet in the palms of my hands and gripped them tightly because it helped to slow the throbbing. I remembered stories from the Bible that Edna had told me, stories of saints who'd gone barefoot into the wilderness to look for wisdom. How had they kept their feet from burning on the hot sand?

Edna had once told me that ancient people made sandals out of plants, out of leaves. I would try to do this. But I needed a plant with enough wide leaves to weave a pair of sandals.

There were no plants around but the kind with spines and twiggy leaves, like sagebrush, cactus, and yucca. There was no water, no way to quench the pain in my feet or the thirst in my throat.

I looked around again. The quietness was not menacing. Instead of being afraid, I was overcome with a certainty of how safe I was. Safe in the dry desert without water—far, far from home, with no place to go, and alone. It seemed crazy. Maybe I was going mad from the heat.

I shook my head and started to cry. Tears came from eyes that I thought were too dry for crying. How stingingly hot they felt, and swollen. Tears streamed and I rubbed my cheeks with my palms. I tasted the salt with my tongue, licking it like a cat licks her paws when she cleans herself.

I wasn't going mad. I was beginning to see what was

true. I was starting to see plainly what had been hidden out of sight. Daddy was a bully. Michelle was a bully. Lito described her perfectly, and Lito described my father in the same moment. I saw my father and Michelle, side by side, as if they belonged to each other. I wasn't his daughter; she was.

I could die today, this afternoon, I thought, tonight, or tomorrow. What would Edna and Bill think if they saw where I was, and what was happening? I couldn't imagine it. No picture came to mind. I could see only my father's bully face, his angry eyes, and Michelle's perfectly unstained teeth.

Another picture replaced the two faces. It was a tree, a slender greenish tree with wide leaves drooping from its branches.

I knew that trees other than the scraggly piñon pine and juniper grew in low places. If I could find a low spot, an arroyo or a sinkhole, I'd find a tree with enough leaves to make leaf sandals.

I walked—hobbled was more like it—until I came to the head of a wash that fell away into the desert plain, twisting like a snake. I went along it. I passed a dried-up waterhole. I was tempted to stop and rub the smooth, dried patches of mud I saw there, as they gleamed like china in the sun. I did that at home when I found dried mud. The surface always felt like velvet under your fingertips.

But I kept going because there was a tree not far ahead. The tree appeared as if in a dream, hazy and stunted. It was a small cottonwood with slender branches and leaves that barely twitched in the breeze that was starting to come up.

I sat in the shade of the tree and rested. The breeze had some life to it. As I felt it brush across my skin, I also felt relief. I began making my sandals.

The cottonwood leaves were stiff and dry with heat, but I could lace and weave them. Making the soles was the easiest part. The leaves seemed designed to lay over and around each other, as if it were part of a plan. I finished one sole and started another. I decided to use the stringy fibers from the leaf blades of a yucca to tie everything together. My sandals were crude, but they stayed on when I walked.

I traveled in a circle that day. I went north, then west, then south and a little east, and returned to the rim of the Canyon in the late afternoon. The thirst and pain of the hours that had passed since morning were changed into memory by the time I was halfway back.

The breeze had swelled into a thunderstorm wind. It pushed against my back, drying the dampness under my hair and behind my ears. Late-afternoon clouds churned up along the eastern horizon. The massed thunderheads growled like a stomach gone empty too long.

The rain pelted the sand and made deep round holes. As the rain got heavier, the clouds were lit with flashes of blue-green lightning. Wide, wet patches began to grow on the parched ground. Then rivers of brown mud swelled and crept like lava.

The trail I'd taken to leave the Canyon was a dry river bed; it became a rushing torrent that dissolved and consumed my sandals and carried the remains away.

The wind drove the rain hard, with a smell almost too sweet to bear. It drenched my body until I became a swimmer, reaching and pulling with my arms.

The rain was gone before sunset. The sky was cleared by big high winds that blew from the northeast. Thunder kept rumbling for a long time, even after the storm was over.

I arrived in camp after everyone else had returned from what they'd been doing that day. "You stumble like an old woman," Dora said. "Help me with supper. Where have you been? I haven't seen you since dawn. Rita has been asking for you."

I helped her with the food, limping and wincing because my feet hurt. I told her where I'd been, about the walking, the heat, the animals I'd seen. "I wasn't afraid of the rattlesnake," I said. "It slithered away and paid no attention to me."

Rita grabbed me around the waist, hugging me tight. She looked at my feet and began shouting that she could see blood.

Dora bent her head down to look closely at my feet. Then she stopped what she was doing and turned aside, summoning me to follow. We went to her bed place and she took a tin of ointment from a cloth bag. Rita watched, silent for a change.

"It is good to respect the rattlesnake for how dangerous it is," Dora said. "Rita, get water. Be quick. Use the small soup pot. Don't trip and spill it on your way back here."

I knew Dora wouldn't ask questions. She'd wait for me to explain. She treated my feet by washing them and smearing them with an ointment that was mostly lard. She wrapped them with rags. I rubbed my eyes when tears came.

Rita held one of my hands and whispered encouraging words. "Don't worry," she said. "You'll be good as new before you know it."

I knew Rita's words were those she had heard many times from her mother and sisters when she had needed bandaging.

Dora took care of my feet and I told her about the two faces I'd imagined seeing: Michelle's and my father's. I tried to tell her how it felt to see my father that way, not as a god roaring thunder but just as a bully.

"You have done *hazhntaago*," she said.

"What's that?"

"I am giving you the Navajo word for something the Plains Indians do, maybe before a fight. It means you want to see something in your mind that you need to see to be brave, to be happy. It is a journey, sometimes taken only in your mind and your thoughts, and at other times with body and mind together."

Dora spoke in a monotone that was so low I could barely hear her. She spoke of sadness, of how it comes before understanding trouble. She knew what had happened to me that day, and she did not act surprised. She even knew the word for it.

Dora loaned me a pair of David Sr.'s socks to cover the rags on my feet. It wasn't hard to walk, now that my skin was layered and protected. I limped, but not too badly.

At the supper fire, Linda and the others wanted to know why I'd been stupid enough to walk such a long time in the desert without shoes. I told them how I'd made sandals with leaves. Their silence, after I told them, showed me they were impressed.

"Where are the sandals you made?" Rita demanded to know. "I want to try them on. I don't care if they're too big. I want to wear them."

"They fell apart in the rain," I said. "I'll make you a pair, ones that fit."

Rita flopped down into my lap, being careful not to bump against my feet.

I watched Jake's face across the fire. I wanted to see what his eyes might say. One side of his mouth was turned up into a half smile.

He noticed me staring and he said, "Michelle came looking for you."

"What did she want?" I saw a flash, for half an instant, of her jeering face.

"Another race. She says she's sorry she cheated. She wants you to race her again."

"What did you say?"

"That you won't race her because she cheats. I said you don't trust her."

"I don't trust her, you're right," I told him.

Somewhere in the fine lines and planes of Jake's face I saw a change. His eyes met mine for an instant—the look in them was softer than before.

Still, I was thinking that something about Michelle made me want to figure her out. I didn't say this to Jake.

"Help me with the dishes, Lito. You, too, Jake." Dora's voice slipped gently through the twilight. Dora never raised her voice.

"I wonder if she means it, about another race," I said, watching Jake.

He didn't answer. He got up and walked over to help his mother haul water for the dish washing. His shoulders seemed stiff. I had the feeling there was something he wanted to say, but he wasn't saying it.

Rita was eager for a story that night.

I made one up about a young horse, a colt, that gets lost in a thunderstorm. After a long search, his mother finds him, safe and sound. Rita wanted to hear the story three times.

Finally she fell asleep, her small chest rising and falling in rhythm with her breathing. That night Rita must have dreamed of being a pony, the way her legs and arms thrashed. I dreamed of frogs, because their croaking voices were the last thing I heard before I slept.

I woke up to Rita yelling in my ear. "Hurry," she said, shaking me. "A wagon is coming into camp."

BERTHA JIM

Danny Watchman wheeled into camp in a wagon that carried a single passenger, an old woman who sat hunched next to the driver. A scarf was wrapped closely around her head and shoulders. Her chin was visible as it rested on a drugstore cane with a shiny, fake-brass covering on the handle.

Rita shouted that "Uncle Nephew" was coming. Danny Watchman was one of Dora's nephews.

The passenger was Bertha Jim, the oldest great-grandmother anybody knew. She was a relation on Dora's side. Bertha Jim was introduced, one by one, to the children. She was thin as a scarecrow and shrunken with age, but her black eyes flashed. Her skin was like crinkly brown paper stretched over a skeletal frame.

Rita took the old woman's gnarled hand and dropped into a curtsy. I wondered where she'd learned to do that. From televison, maybe, or magazines. Rita gazed into the old woman's face with a fierce intensity.

I knew Rita's thoughts. "What does it feel like to be as old as you?" she was asking wordlessly. "Can you still have fun?"

David Sr. helped Bertha Jim to a wooden bench in the shade under the cottonwoods, where she could rest and still be a part of the company.

Dora positioned herself next to Bertha Jim on the bench. "My girls will fix a bed for you in the wagon," Dora said. "You'll be comfortable there. It's too hot and stuffy to sleep in the hogan." We went to work fixing the bed while the two women sat talking.

When Bertha Jim spoke English, it was with a strong accent. She interrupted her English with Navajo words and phrases. I barely knew Navajo, but the way she spoke, gesturing with her hands and arms, left no doubt about her meaning.

She was tired from her journey into the Canyon, she said. Journeys into the Canyon were hard on an old woman. Dora nodded sympathetically. "I loved coming to the Canyon as a girl," Bertha Jim said, "with all of my relatives. They're gone now, dead or too far away for me to see anymore."

We rushed to get things ready, grabbing pillows and rugs to pad a sleeping place for her in the wagon. She clutched her cane with both hands and leaned forward, using the cane for leverage. Her eyes were focused on the trees beyond the open area of the camp. The look on her face made me imagine she was expecting someone of importance to emerge from the shadows.

I liked her right away. It wasn't just that she was very old. (I had the general feeling that very old people were wise and kind.) It was the sharpness of her tongue. She reminded me of Bill's wife, Edna. The way she talked about the dust in her nose during the wagon ride was real enough to make me sneeze. She spoke in a monotone, the same way Dora did. Her voice drifted with the heat and insect noise of the morning. There was no beginning or end to it.

I paused to slap at the no-see-ums that were biting my wrists. Bertha Jim turned from her conversation with Dora. "Look," she said to me, one arm raised to catch my attention. "You can't stop the biting unless you jump in the water and smear yourself with mud. Go jump in the water!"

I did what she said, smearing my skin with mud, and the insects stopped biting.

When the old one's bed was ready, she nodded in approval. "I will sleep tonight in the bed you have made for me," she said, "and be comfortable even with my bad dreams."

I wanted to ask what she meant about bad dreams, but I was too shy.

Dora turned to Linda and me and asked us to go pick up some corn for supper from a neighboring family who grew enough corn to sell it extra cheaply. She said, "Get peaches, too, but only the ripe ones in the orchard. Take Rita so she won't be underfoot."

The peach orchard belonged to the Wilsons, so Dora

handed Linda the right amount of money for just the corn. To carry the corn and peaches, Linda got a cloth bag with a shoulder strap. The three of us set off. Linda and Rita knew the way, so I followed them.

Rita twirled along, barefoot on the sand. Her short, stocky body was spinning, with her hands clasped over her head. "I'm a dancer on the stage," she announced.

I walked next to Linda so I could ask about Bertha Jim. Many visitors came and went from camp, but there was something special and different about the old woman. Maybe Linda could tell me what it was.

"Tell me about Bertha Jim." I asked, "Who is she, exactly?"

"She's a Medicine Woman. We have a few. Navajo medicine people are usually men. She is so old, most of her family members are dead or scattered. It's hard for her to visit them," Linda said.

Rita stopped dancing long enough to interrupt. "Tell Jamie where Bertha Jim was born. Say that part."

Linda grabbed for a loose strand of Rita's hair. "You baby," she said, laughing. She reached to catch Rita's shoulders, and a game of chase started. "You're always asking questions and ordering people around. Why can't you be quiet for one second?"

Linda ended the chase while Rita kept going. The lines on Linda's face relaxed into seriousness.

"Bertha Jim was born near Black Mesa, a mountain that is sacred to the Navajo people. She misses her birthplace. It's *ho' dizhchiigi*. That's a word that means where a person is born." Linda pronounced the Navajo word haltingly, stretching the syllables.

Rita had been listening. She ran to her sister and grabbed Linda's T-shirt in her hands. She jumped up and down, tugged on the shirt, and yelled, "Tell about the placenta!"

"The what?" I asked.

"When a baby is born, its mother buries the afterbirth and the cord under a tree or maybe next to a sheep corral. Wherever it is, the spot will be important to the child. For as long as the child lives, it matters to him or her. Bertha is sad because she's old and lonely. She's far from the place where her cord is buried."

"Does everybody do that?" I asked. "Bury the cord?"

"Yes, if they are keeping the old ways, the traditions," Linda answered. "My mother buried all of ours in different places close to home."

"How did Bertha Jim become a Medicine Woman, if usually only men can?"

"Her father was a great Medicine Man. Her grandfather was, too. She learned from them. It was plain when she was still a tiny child, like Rita, that she had special healing gifts and powers."

Linda's softly spoken words conjured up pictures in my mind. I imagined Bertha Jim running along the wash barefoot, a four-year-old girl as wild and free as Rita.

"Why did she come to camp now, do you think?"

"I'm not sure," Linda answered, wrinkling her brow. "I guess we'll find out."

Our conversation ended as we neared the neighbor's sheep camp.

Next to Dora, Linda was the Wilson most likely to answer my questions. However, there were rare times when even she wearied of my curiosity and wouldn't answer.

The neighbor, Sally Blackgoat, gave us ears of corn with the husks still on. She packed these in our sack. Linda handed over three one-dollar bills. Sally Blackgoat nodded and smiled.

"Come back again," she said, as we walked away.

I offered to carry the corn. We walked past the Blackgoats' hogan and their herd of sheep grazing in a meadow. We circled around to the right and headed in the direction of the Wilsons' peach orchard.

The air under the peach trees was heavy with flies. We slapped at them, or brushed them away, as we picked all the ripe fruit we could find. Rita climbed a tree to get at the peaches that were too high for us to reach from the ground.

On the way back I tried to ask more questions about Bertha Jim. Linda's expression told me she wanted to keep her thoughts to herself. She didn't feel like talking.

During the days that followed I stared at Bertha Jim whenever I could. She was bent over like a willow, with a bony hump between her shoulder blades. When she pronounced her thoughts about things in a conversation, her arms and hands swiped the air. She was constantly gesturing. Her movements made me think of flickering insects.

Her washed-out red cotton skirt had many folds. She wore a dark blue cotton blouse. Her buckskin moccasins had silver buttons on the sides, and she wore white cotton athletic socks. Three silver necklaces were strung around her neck. On four reedy fingers she had bright silver rings with turquoise stones.

Her hair was looped in a bun and held at the back of her neck by a thick silver clasp studded with turquoise. In spite of her age, her hair was mostly black with only a few gray streaks.

I'd never seen such a wrinkled face, not even on a new-born pig. Creases cut deep into her skin around her eyes and mouth like canyons. Her skin was the color of charred wood.

One time she caught me staring, but she didn't scold. "You've never seen anyone so old? That is right, yes?" she asked.

"Yes," I answered, lowering my eyes.

"No grandfather or grandmother?"

"One of my grandmothers died last year. She lived in Chicago, Illinois. I hardly ever saw her. Once in a while we'd take the train and go see her and Grandpa. It takes two days on the train. My grandfather is still alive. And then I have another grandmother in another place, but it's just as far—Indianapolis, Indiana. But I don't think any of them are as old as you."

"Ah," the old woman sighed. "Tell me what you know about these people."

I told her everything I knew about my grandparents. I told her that Grandpa was a banker, and that one Grandma lost her wits and died not knowing who she was, and that my other Grandma was raised poor and made a widow when my father was ten years old. "Daddy had to go to work, then," I said, frowning. An image of my father as a boy simmered in my mind, then went away.

"I've never seen anybody as old as you, though." By now

I was looking at her directly, with my eyes on hers. "How old are you? Is it okay to ask?"

"Okay," she said, grinning. She had almost no teeth in her mouth. "Curiosity is good," she said. "I am more than one hundred, but I don't know for sure anymore. Like that grandmother of yours, my wits are going."

I didn't know what to say. I stood in front of her, gazing into her eyes.

Looking directly back at me she said, "Why does it matter to you, child? These numbers of years?"

Uncertain what to say, I told her I liked old people.

"Why?"

"They're kind," I said. I was thinking of some of the grand-fathers and grandmothers of my friends at home. "And they tell stories. My Grandpa tells me stories whenever I see him."

Bertha Jim tapped the ground gently with the bottom of her cane. "You are unusual for a white girl, thinking this way."

Her words surprised me because I hadn't thought of myself as a white girl for many days and nights now.

Dora interrupted our talk by offering each of us a chunk of fry bread smeared with honey. The old woman jawed her food with enthusiasm. As honey ran down her chin, she wiped at the drip with the sleeve of her blouse. Our conversation was over. Her attention had moved to the food.

Three days after Bertha Jim came into camp we all gathered under the cottonwoods around the supper fire. We ate a meal prepared in the old woman's honor. The girls helped Dora fix mutton stew with carrots and potatoes, fry bread with honey, and coffee with cream and sugar. Rita got to drink several cans of her favorite soda, black cherry.

After the meal, the younger children cleaned up while the adults talked. Then all of us sat in the quiet and some people told stories. Jake described tracking a pair of coyotes along the wash and finding their den with pups inside.

"We hear that pair nearly every night," David Jr. said.

"I've seen them myself," Rita said. "The babies, anyway."

"No you haven't," Jake said, smiling at his little sister. "More tall tales."

The fire burned low. I was having trouble staying awake, but I didn't want to miss anything. It was a frog-noisy night, with crickets, too. I concentrated on the cadence of the cricket chirps. I became alert suddenly when Dora spoke of a ceremony.

"We'll have a Blessingway to bring back your strength," she said, speaking to Bertha Jim. "I know a Medicine Man at Many Farms. We'll get him here."

"A Medicine Man is expensive," Bertha said. "I can't pay. I have no money anymore."

"No need for that," David Sr. said. "We'll bring him here. And we'll pay him. Our peach crop was good last summer and better this year. This is something we can do for you. We'll have the ceremony as soon as he can come."

The old woman gulped her coffee out of a tin cup. She made wet sounds with her tongue and lips. She smiled and, for a moment, in the firelight, she looked like an ancient baby, toothless and wrinkled. "You're generous," she said. "Kind to an old woman."

"I know this man," Dora said. "He's very good, and worth the money he asks. He does this Blessingway and one or two others. I've seen him. I can vouch for him."

"My sadness has been a terrible thing," Bertha Jim said quietly. "I'm too old to struggle with it. The Blessingway will be good. It will help."

"We'll have a feast afterward," David Sr. said. "We'll roast a lamb."

The old woman chuckled. The sound was somewhere between a chicken scratching dry ground and paper rustling. "I will be hungry afterward for lamb," she said with a grin.

Bill had once described a Blessingway ceremony to me. I knew there were different ceremonies for men and women. I remembered him saying that Blessingway ceremonies are expensive—that a Medicine Man trains all his life, from when he's a little boy, and that he asks to be paid well for his work.

The fire went out. Everyone wandered away to their sleeping places. David Jr. and Jake helped Bertha Jim into her bed in the wagon. Dora headed for her own bed, the one she shared with David Sr. I tucked Rita in and went to find Dora. She was walking silently into the trees, toward the outhouse. I reached out to touch her arm and whispered her name.

"What is it?" she said, turning.

"I want to ask you something." It was dark and I could hardly see Dora's face in the shadows. "I want to give you money to help pay the Medicine Man. Will you let me? I know from Bill that they're expensive, and Bertha Jim just said so."

"Why?" Dora asked. "Why would you give me money for this?"

"I want him to sing for me, too."

She didn't answer right away. She was thinking about my question. The light of a half moon fell on her face. She thought for a long time. Chirping crickets and the scufflings of rodents filled my ears.

"You don't understand," she said at last.

"What don't I understand?"

"What has Bill said about Blessingway ceremonies?"

I searched my mind for the details. "He said Medicine Men study all their lives and need to be paid well. He said they come to cure sadness, the kind Bertha Jim has, loneliness. I want him to sing for me, too."

"Do you believe the Medicine Man's songs will help you? Is this something you believe? Have you thought about it?"

"I have thought about it," I said in a strong voice. Panic rose in my throat. Would I be refused? Would they keep me away because I was a white girl?

"If you have belief, then you will know a difference and feel better after the songs in the ceremony," she said softly.

"Please let me give you some money."

"I don't want your money."

"What can I give you? What can I do that would help?"

"Help us get ready. There are things to do. Rita needs a bath. And her hair needs to be washed. You need the same, and so do the other girls."

"Okay," I said. "If that's all."

I started to walk away, feeling self-conscious and confused.

"Wait," Dora said. "Listen. The Blessingway is for an old woman who is sad because she's far from her birthplace.

She's suffered many losses. She seeks *hozho*. It's hard to explain *hozho*, but I say it means having a balance between happiness and sadness. It is peace. Bertha Jim looks for peace. I understand why you want to offer something, to be a part of this. It's because there is trouble in your family."

Dora paused, as if gathering her thoughts.

"You are not Navajo. This means certain things. But you are a part of us, our family, and so you are a part of the Blessingway. We would make this ceremony for you, if it was plain you needed it. You are not closed out, do you understand?"

"Yes," I told her, not certain it was true. "I think so."

"Come to the ceremony with an open spirit, open wide like the desert. The ceremony is for you, for me, for all of us. Something might happen when you hear the songs. Even if you don't know what everything means, remember how I have told you of *hozho*."

Then Dora laughed, a smooth rippling sound. She took my hand and held it lightly.

"You are one of us, a relation. This is how we think of you. We don't want your money. It means nothing. If you travel a way of beauty, if you smile and are glad to be alive, this is what matters to us, to David, to Rita and the other children, and to me. What we wish for ourselves we wish for you."

"I am lucky Bertha Jim has come into camp and there will be a Blessingway for her."

"Yes, in some ways I would call you lucky," Dora said, smiling and rubbing my hand between her two warm ones. "Now go to bed."

A BLESSINGWAY CEREMONY

Preparations for the ceremony started at dawn the next day. David Jr. rode to Many Farms to make a deal with the Medicine Man. Three days later he rode back into camp followed by an old man on a big roan horse.

The Medicine Man wore a preacher's black coat and a black felt hat with a band made of conchos. His gray hair was draped around his shoulders like feathers. He didn't smile when he was greeted. Rita was afraid of him. She hid behind Dora, peering cautiously around her mother's skirts, and stared with huge dark eyes.

The ceremony began at dawn the following morning.

The eight-sided hogan had been made ready. Brilliantly colored rugs covered the dirt floor. The bedding and other family possessions that were usually piled up against the inside walls had been removed and placed in the wagon beds. When the sun's bright warmth came over the rim of the Canyon, the Medicine Man entered the hogan with Bertha Jim behind him.

The Medicine Man was tall and broad shouldered. He stooped to keep from hitting the door frame with his head. He had removed his felt hat.

Dora and her daughters, several women from other camps, and Rita and I, she holding my hand, all filed in. Each of us circled the hogan interior once, in a clockwise direction, before sitting down. The Medicine Man and Bertha were seated in the center of the hazy shadowed room, next to the oil drum stove.

It was a woman's ceremony. No men were permitted.

The singing began. The Medicine Man's voice had a range from a deep rumble, like water flowing, to a shrill whine that made me think of bats flying through the air at high speed.

There was no melody to the singing. The sounds were ancient. They echoed off the hogan walls and slid through the air like smoke does when there is no wind.

We listened and watched. The soft wool of the blankets under us made comfortable padding. Light slipped down through the smoke hole in the roof, revealing the expressions on the faces of everyone present.

The Medicine Man's gestures were trancelike and deliberate. He removed all of Bertha Jim's clothes, exposing her naked body. He took off her moccasins and socks. Her toes were twisted with arthritis. When he had removed all of her clothing and jewelry, he turned his attention away from her.

He pulled two small leather pouches out of his coat pocket. From one he took a white carrot-shaped root. I recognized it as yucca root because Dora used it to make soap.

One of the women got up and left the hogan. No one spoke—she just went as if she knew to go without being told. In a few minutes she was back with a large bowl of water. Carefully she handed the bowl to the Medicine Man. She didn't spill a drop.

He dipped the white root into the water and scrubbed until he had a bubbly froth of soapsuds. He began to wash the old woman's body. He covered every inch of her, including her scalp and hair, the spaces between her toes and fingers, and even her creased and wrinkled face. He never stopped chanting.

I stared at his hands. I understood now what it was like to have your sorrows washed away. Even I, a white girl, could feel the peace created by the singing, the washing, and the company of people you liked all around you.

The Medicine Man finished washing Bertha Jim and began to wash her skirt, blouse, moccasins, jewelry, and socks.

Time moved like a heartbeat with a regular pulse. There were moments I feared I'd doze off and miss something. It was smotheringly hot. The steady throb of the songs and the mesmerizing voice of the Medicine Man made me sleepy.

The Medicine Man's singing was like a visible bright thread in front of me. The thread connected his gestures with the sounds he made until a whole piece of imaginary fabric emerged.

Rita slept. Her damp sticky arms lay across my lap. The passing of the hours didn't matter. Light came in through the smoke hole and shifted gradually as the sun traveled across the sky.

I stopped worrying about sleep. My senses became sharper as the hours crawled by. In some mysterious way, the washing seemed like it might have been happening to me as well as to Bertha Jim.

The Medicine Man finished washing Bertha Jim's possessions. Then he drew pinches of pollen from his second pouch. The pollen was yellowish white. It was like the kind bumblebees carry around on their legs. He sprinkled the pollen on the old woman's body—her hair, shoulders, backside, and breasts. She changed color from a creased brown to a shimmering white.

When she was completely covered with pollen, the Medicine Man stood up. While still singing he grasped her under the elbows and pulled her upright. He took a long moment to let her find some strength in her weak legs. He stood next to her and put his arm around her, as a grown son would his mother. Then, with his two strong arms, he lifted her up, with her back resting in one of his arms and her legs on the other, and carried her through the low hogan door. She was so tiny, like a bird, and mostly bones. I almost cried out, fearing that some piece of her would break.

The Medicine Man's chant ceased the instant he stepped into the light of evening. It was near sunset, and soon it would be dark. We had been inside the hogan for the entire day.

The old woman was placed gently on a blanket by the stream. Once she was settled comfortably, the Medicine Man walked away to join the other men and boys who were preparing a meal.

Bertha Jim was dressed by Dora and some of the other women and given water to drink. The women and girls scurried around the old woman like hens, making sure she had what she needed.

All of Bertha Jim's clothing was new—it had been purchased by Dora in town. It was wrapped in tissue and pulled from a box with the store's name on it. The jewelry she'd been wearing earlier was returned to her fingers and neck. Her hair was rewound into a bun and held in place by the same silver clasp.

We drank water from the mouth of a plastic jug. The water revived my awareness of the physical world around me. I'd become lost in the chants, the smells, the sights, and the sounds of the Blessingway. To come out of it, to gulp cold, sweet lemonade that Dora had made the day before, kept on ice that David Jr. had gotten in town, was like waking from a dream.

Rita, who was bursting with energy after her long nap, wanted to play in the river. As I followed her, the sharp aroma of roasting lamb met my nose. My stomach growled, reminding me that we hadn't eaten since supper the night before.

Rita tugged on my arms and then ran around behind me to push on my rump. "You're a slowpoke," she shouted. Rita had dashed into the stream and was splashing furiously when Linda and some of the other girls joined us. Before long a water game was in progress, with everybody getting completely soaked. When the game slowed, we waded out further to squish our toes in the bottom mud and talk.

Rita dipped her hands into the mud and turned to smear

me with it. When I whirled around to capture her, I saw Michelle. She stood, by herself, in a pattern of shadows cast by a clump of willows. She was watching us.

"Hello," I said. I smiled. I didn't know what else to do.

She didn't say anything at first. She took a few steps forward and came to where we were playing in the mud. She was barefoot and wearing rolled-up blue jeans and a dirty white T-shirt. I was surprised at how filthy her shirt was.

"Shake hands?" Michelle said to me. Her face was like a mask.

"What for?" I asked.

"The race," she answered shyly. Her brow lowered. I could plainly see it was hard for her to be asking me to shake hands, to make amends. "I couldn't let you win. I just couldn't," she tried to explain.

Behind me Rita was yanking on my shirt. She whispered words I could make no sense of. I hushed her.

"Okay," I said, reaching out to shake Michelle's hand. Her hand was cool and wet. She had a strong, almost painful grip.

"What'd you do that for?" Rita whispered loudly.

"Be quiet," I told her.

"I meant to come to the Blessingway," Michelle said. Her voice had none of the brashness I remembered. Her eyes were beautiful, with a slant to them. For a second I envied how pretty she was.

"You knew about it?"

"Everybody in the Canyon knows. I was in Window Rock with my uncles. I wish I could have come here instead."

"What'd you do in Window Rock?" I asked the question

to make conversation. I didn't honestly care what she'd done that day.

"Don't ask her things," Rita squealed behind me.

"Rita, be quiet," I said. "Just for a minute."

"It doesn't matter. I didn't do anything anyway."

"That's a lie," Rita said in a loud, accusing voice. "I bet you had snuff and drank whiskey."

"You can't say things like that, Rita, unless you know they're true," I scolded.

"I do know they're true," Rita insisted. "Everybody does."

"I don't do those things," Michelle said. "Who told you I do?"

"Jake," Rita said. "And my father, and David Jr. They've all seen you."

Rita spoke with conviction. It was hard to know what was a lie and what was true. I was relieved when Lito, Jake, and Linda splashed over to say supper was ready.

"Come eat?" I said to Michelle. I ignored Jake's hard stare when he caught sight of us talking.

Michelle turned and walked away without answering.

Each day for a week Michelle came to stand in the stream by the willows. I went to meet her each time. At first Rita was dismayed, and didn't know what to think. But she soon forgot her original anger and played while Michelle and I talked.

Michelle never played games. And she wouldn't eat with us. She talked, that was all. She told me small details about her life. Not once did she show the bold bullying behavior I'd seen the first times we met.

One night she asked me how I came to be in the Canyon. I thought about telling her the truth, but I didn't tell her. Jake had warned me not to trust her, yet I was beginning to. She didn't look evil. Her ways were strange, but I was starting to like her.

At supper one night that same week Linda said to me, "She thinks the world is against her. That's what she thinks."

"I wonder why," I said.

"If you try to make friends with her, she'll ruin it. She's like that."

"Do you believe in witches?" I asked Linda. "Jake does. He thinks Michelle might be one."

"She might be," Linda said. "She could be." Linda shrugged as if it didn't matter to her, one way or another.

Rita, who always listened in, said, "Witches are people with bad hearts."

"The kind that are evil," Linda explained. "Not the heart-attack kind."

"They don't even have hearts," Rita said evenly. "That's what's wrong with them."

"Just be careful, like Jake said," Linda told me.

"It's sad, the way she gets treated," I said.

"It's her own fault," Linda replied, and from the way she said it I knew the conversation was over.

Bertha Jim stayed for ten days. Her mood had changed after the Blessingway. The difference was plain in her eyes. She was tranquil now. She sat on the bench under the trees, fanning her face with a paper fan Dora had given her, and looked up at the cottonwood leaves rustling over her head.

When she left, I hugged her as hard as I dared, considering how frail she was. She seemed as much a grandmother to me as any I'd had in my life.

Right before Bertha Jim left, and for one day after, Michelle didn't come. I wondered why. I went looking for her, and as I peered into the willows, I expected her to jump out at me any second.

On a breathlessly hot afternoon, one day after lunch, she was there, ambling along as if she had a million years to travel a quarter mile. I ran to meet her.

"Why did you stop coming?" I asked.

"I went to town, that's all."

"Where do you live? I've never seen your place, or I might have gone there to find you."

"Want to come now?"

"Sure," I said. "Let's go."

We walked for about a mile and then made a left turn around a towering rock wall and walked some more. We climbed over a wooden fence that was so old it was falling down, and finally we came to Michelle's camp.

It was mid-afternoon. A fire was burning in an oil drum. It was the trash set ablaze. The smoke coiling up through the trees had a nasty stink to it. Two women, both of them much older than Dora, sat on the ground under a big cottonwood tree not far from the oil drum. They were busy picking thorns and stickers out of a large pile of sheep wool. The wool, more yellow than white, was the color of unsalted butter. The women were dressed in the old style. Both wore kerchiefs tied around their heads.

When we walked up, one of the women said hello. The second one didn't speak. Instead she looked up and smiled halfheartedly. She then dropped her gaze back to the work she was doing.

"You must be the white girl Michelle told us about," the speaking woman said. "You're staying with the Wilsons, yes?"

"Yes," I said, wondering what Michelle had told them. I felt the other girl's body tensing as she stood next to me.

"You're welcome any time," the woman said. The other one didn't look up again. She kept her chin down, her eyes focused on the bits of stuff she was pulling from the wool.

A dog, as thin as any I'd ever seen, hung behind the two women and growled slightly. The dog looked pitiful, with burrs in its fur and every rib sticking out.

Michelle didn't say my name or introduce me. Using one raised shoulder, she gestured that I was to follow her. We walked into a field in back of the shadehouse—there was a hogan sheltered under the trees. We stood among a herd of about twenty sheep. A small boy was waving a stick in our direction. His face was like Michelle's, with the same beautifully slanted eyes. He was happy to see us—his face broke into a wide smile.

"Is he your brother?" I asked, looking at the boy.

"My cousin," Michelle said. Her face had a tender, gentle look on it, a look I'd never seen her have before. "He's my mother's sister's boy. He lives with us in the summer."

I wanted to ask who "us" meant, and was about to, when the boy launched himself into Michelle's arms.

"Norman, say hello to Jamie."

"Hello Jamie," Norman said. Then he asked Michelle, "Is she the white girl you said about? With the horse? Jake's friend?"

"Yes," Michelle said. She caught my look and I knew she

119

was embarrassed. "She's the one I told you about, the one who is a good rider."

I wondered, again, about what Jake had said. Watch out for Michelle. Michelle is a witch. She can't be trusted. Was she being nice so she could turn around and be cruel?

"Sit down," Michelle said to me, while pointing to the ground. Her tone was bossy, but not unkind.

I dropped down and almost instantly felt the press of curious sheep all around. The smell of them was potent—a mixture of ammonia, bad breath, the oils in their wool, and dust.

Michelle sat down, pushing hard at the bodies of the sheep that wanted, it seemed, to surround us completely. Michelle spoke to the sheep as if they were human. She called out their names, scolding them as one would children. Norman held his small, straight back against the side of one animal. He was about to be knocked over when Michelle grabbed him and stood up. She yelled at the sheep in a shrill, mean voice. It was the old Michelle, the one I knew.

The sheep scattered. Soon they were grazing peacefully again, the way they were when we had arrived in the meadow.

"You went to the Blessingway. How come?" she asked out of the blue. It wasn't the question I expected.

"I wanted to," I said. "Dora told me I was welcome. I wanted to see if the songs would make me feel different." I stopped speaking, unable to finish. Shyness and a reluctance to trust Michelle blocked the words I might have said.

"Why does it matter to you? Did you like it?" Michelle did not wait for an answer. Her words came like shots, one after another. "You're like me. You're an outcast. Nobody wants you. I found out about you from somebody who knows. You can be my friend because we're the same, we're both outcasts."

Michelle's eyes narrowed. The softness in them belied her words. I wondered who had told her about me. She stared, waiting for a reply.

"Who told you nobody wants me?"

"Joe, the man who took you to see your mother. He's one of my uncles. He told his wife, Stella, and my cousin, who is eight, listened. Everybody wondered about you when you came. My cousin finally told me what he knew after I gave him a dollar. The Wilsons wouldn't talk. It was only Joe who knew. Once he told Stella, everybody knew."

Michelle smiled. Her whole face could change from lovely to ugly, depending on the words she formed with her mouth, lips, and tongue.

"How come you're an outcast?" I asked defensively.

"My mother sold me on the street in Gallup, to some people who wanted a baby."

I didn't believe her. I looked away, refusing to meet her eyes. I shook my head and sighed. Michelle did not say any more. I knew she was trying to shock me. It wasn't true. It was a stupid lie.

"Who are those women over there? Picking the wool?"

"My grandmother is the one who speaks. The other one has been deaf since she was a kid. She's my aunt. I live with my grandmother and grandfather. They take care of me."

She sounded truthful and sincere. The look on her face was only slightly jeering. Maybe she was telling the truth.

"How come your mother sold you?" I asked.

"For booze. She was a drunk."

"Was?"

"She died when I was seven."

"How old are you now?"

"Same as you, twelve and a half."

"How come you know my exact age?"

"I just do, that's all," Michelle said. She rose to her feet, dusting off her already grubby clothing. "Let's go," she said. "Come on, Norman, you come, too. The sheep aren't going to wander. I know a secret place where there's a cave."

I hesitated, not sure if I wanted to be with her. I pictured Michelle as a tiny wrapped bundle being handed over on a street in Gallup—an exchange of a baby for five hundred dollars, seven hundred, a thousand. What was a baby worth?

Michelle loped away, dragging Norman by one thin arm. I expected him to complain, but instead he got into stride and ran like a little rabbit. We crossed the sheep meadow, slid under a section of ancient wooden fence, and raced across the bottom of the Canyon to the other side. We ran along the base of a sandstone wall and stopped when we came to a deep cut in the rock, a slot canyon.

"I know as many secret places as Jake does, maybe more," Michelle bragged. She squeezed her body through the opening to the slot canyon. "Come on, there's a surprise up in here. I'll show you if you promise not to tell anybody."

Intrigued, I followed her. Once we passed through the opening, the narrow slit in the sandstone opened up enough so we could walk normally, with our arms swinging alongside our hips. The thick atmosphere in the tunnellike cut was damp and sweet-smelling, reminding me of fresh grass after rain.

"This way," Michelle called out in a whispery voice. She turned to me for an instant and placed one finger to her mouth, warning me to be still. She turned sharply and began to follow the sandy bottom of the canyon. Norman said nothing, but darted close to Michelle's heels.

"Does Jake know this place?" I asked.

"Maybe," Michelle answered. "Maybe not. It's my private, secret place. I come here when I'm sick of those old women back there." Even when Michelle was being nice there could be an edge to what she said.

We walked in silence for about twenty minutes. Then the cut widened slightly and Michelle rushed ahead. I lost sight of her. Seconds later, I heard her calling from somewhere above my head.

I stood still and looked up. At first all I could see was the blue slice of sky overhead because my eyes were blinded by a purplish glow coming off the sandstone. It was the sun's reflected light. Then I saw where she was. Her small figure was crouched in the entrance to a shallow cave roughly twenty feet above me. Norman had disappeared from view.

"How'd you get up there?"

"Easy," Michelle answered. "If you know the way, that is."

"Show me."

With her right arm, Michelle pointed out a trail that wound around a bulge of sandstone. "Go that way, then you'll see."

I did what she said. Once beyond the big rock, I saw a

delicate, barely visible series of cuts in the wall, hand and foot holes leading directly to the cave where Michelle, with Norman next to her, sat grinning like a cat. I climbed up to the cave.

It was an amazing place, one that nobody would have dreamed existed. But the Canyon was rich with such hidden, secret alcoves.

We sat for a while in silence. Then Michelle told me a story about how her ancestors cut the holes in the rocks. They were people who lived before the wheel was invented. "And maybe even before fire," she added, with pride in her voice. "This was a sacred place to them. They came here for prayers and rituals."

The way she had been talking made me wonder if she was proud to be Navajo, instead of ashamed, as she sometimes acted.

"You're glad you're Navajo," I said.

"I'm glad now," she said. "It's good to be something, to belong somewhere. Once, I hated being Navajo."

"How come you hated it?"

Michelle got very quiet, as if she needed time to find the right words. "It's because of what I told you, about being sold. When I found out about what happened, I hated everybody for a long time."

Our conversation died. I didn't know what to make of her story, whether to believe or disbelieve it.

"Thanks for showing me your secret place. I need to get back pretty soon," I said.

"You won't tell about the cave?"

"No, I said I wouldn't."

"And you're not allowed to come here alone, only with me and Norman."

"Okay," I said. "I promise."

"Come see me again sometime soon, okay?"

"I will."

We climbed down carefully. Going down was a lot harder than going up because of the slippery nature of the sandstone. Once we were back by the wash, Michelle turned to go.

"Wait," I said.

Michelle stopped and looked at me. Her dark eyes were questioning.

"Do you use snuff?" I asked.

"I did. But not now. What do you care, anyhow?"

"I'm glad you don't, that's all."

Michelle ran off, with Norman leaping behind her. I was relieved to hear her say she didn't use snuff any longer. And for some strange reason I believed her.

I was walking along the Canyon toward camp when I heard a horse and rider coming up from behind. As I glanced back, I knew I'd seen that rider a hundred times before. My chest got tight.

I squatted down on my haunches and waited until the rider was close enough for me to see his eyes in the shadow under the brim of his hat. I jumped up and shouted his name.

"Bill," I called. "It really is you!"

He reined in his horse and looked at me. I stood in the midst of a miniature cloud of dust cast by his horse's feet. "Say now, you look like a native."

"I'm glad to see you," I burst out. I rubbed dust from my eyes.

"Well, I'm glad to see you, too," he said, doffing his hat in my direction.

"Need a ride somewhere?" he asked, as if it were any day of the week and I were taking the dirt road home from a friend's house.

"I won't refuse," I said, laughing.

Bill reached down for my wrist and, with surprising strength for somebody so thin, pulled me up on his horse. I sat on the animal's rump and held the cantle of Bill's leather saddle.

BILL COMES TO
THE CANYON

Nobody in camp acted as if seeing Bill was out of the ordinary. I even wondered if they had known he was on his way and didn't tell me. I knew he and I would have to go somewhere private, away from the others, to talk. I had questions.

The sadness had been out of my chest for a while. When I realized it was gone, I was amazed. I couldn't remember the exact hour or minute it left. Seeing Bill, and being certain of why he came, caused the sadness to seep back like a closed wound bleeding inward.

After supper, Bill asked me to take a ride with him in the Canyon.

"There's a moon," he said, looking up. "It'll be bright as noonday."

"I want to go, too," Rita said, in her most insistent voice.

"Not this time, baby girl," Dora said. She reached for Rita's shoulders with both hands and took her gently into an embrace. "This time you stay here. Let Jamie have time with Bill by herself."

We rode double, like before, on Bill's roan. The horse was small and muscular. He had a dark red coat with a mane trimmed short and a stringy tail. Bill had broken him "Indian style," which meant gently and slowly, with no violence.

We rode for a while without speaking. We listened to the restless night sounds of the Canyon, a place that is never truly still.

The moon made the rocks glow. I looked up and saw the Milky Way, a broad ribbon of stars thrown across the heavens. I pictured us in the Canyon on planet Earth as a part of the wheel of stars, of fires burning. I asked Bill if stars ever go out.

"Sure they do," he answered. "Like anything else, they get used up after a while. But stars take a long time to die."

"Millions of years, or trillions?"

"Both, I expect. Depends on the star."

"Bill, what's going to happen next? Do you know? You came to get me, didn't you? Mother said she'd be sending you. Is that why you came?"

"Yes."

"Please tell me what's happening." My tears were starting.

Bill said, "Let's get down and walk for a while. I can talk to you better that way."

I slid off the horse. The sand was comfortably warm under my feet. Bill swung down and we moved forward again. This time we walked side by side with the horse behind us. The reins dangled from the fingers of Bill's left hand. Noticing which hand Bill used reminded me that he was a lefty.

"First," he said, hesitating, "I want to tell you that Joe has been calling your mother now and then, to say how you've been doing out here, getting along with folks and such. That's something you ought to know."

I nodded without speaking.

"It didn't seem right not to have somebody willing to check in now and then. Joe is a good man. He wasn't spying."

"I know. I don't mind him calling." I remembered the look on Joe's face as he dropped me off after the meeting with my mother. He had taken it all in.

"Good," Bill said, sounding relieved. "Now, the next thing. You're meant to come on back with me. I brought the pickup. It's in Chinle, parked at David's house. We're meant to go on back together, you and me."

So far everything he was telling me sounded fine. I knew the bad part was coming. "Go on."

"Your Daddy is going to Europe with his new wife." Bill paused. I could see it was awful for him, what he had to say. Speaking in his quietest voice, he continued. "You kids, except your brother, are being sent to boarding schools. They have the schools picked out already. Your brother . . . well, he'll live with your mother. Your mother and her new husband—that would be your stepfather—are moving to Albuquerque."

"Albuquerque," I said the word out loud. The way it shaped itself in my mouth offered no meaning, no weight.

"Boarding schools?" I tugged hard on Bill's sleeve. "Where are the schools? How come more than one? Are we all going to different schools? If we go, that is." My mind was a muddle. My words came out sounding like the words of someone learning to speak English.

"The school they picked for you is in California. The one your sisters will go to is in Colorado."

"How come two different ones? Why are they sending me so far away?"

"I can't answer your questions, Jamie. Your daddy made the decision about the schools."

I hated what he was saying. I didn't want to listen. Abruptly my mind swerved to images of the Medicine Man, the old woman, Bertha Jim, her nakedness, the threads I'd imagined weaving together to make a cloth. "I went to a Blessingway," I said.

"Oh?"

I knew I'd caught Bill off guard. I'd interrupted his explanation, his telling of the news. "It was my first time to see one," I added, as if Bill didn't know this. "It felt like being in a dream, only without going to sleep. When it was over, and I went to play with Rita in the water, I could hardly believe a whole day had gone by."

Bill's voice went soft, like it did when he was extra thoughtful. "You felt different afterward, not as you'd felt before, is my guess," Bill said. "Nobody goes to a Blessingway and comes away the same as they were to begin."

"I felt like I was being washed together with Bertha Jim. The songs got inside me. I'll never forget the way they sounded or what the ceremony looked like and smelled like."

I tried to describe to Bill how it was in the hogan, but my mind was playing tricks. Suddenly, without realizing the question was even in my brain, I asked, "Bill, what happens if I don't go back with you?"

"You must, Jamie. The Wilsons would probably let you stay, but is that a good idea? I mean, you do have family."

"What about Daddy? The way he is with me. What about that?"

Bill didn't answer at first. I thought maybe he hadn't heard me. I opened my mouth to ask again when Bill said, "You're better off away from him."

I sighed deeply. This brief but firmly spoken acknowledgment of Daddy's cruelty to me made a difference. It helped me somehow.

"Why can't I be with you and Edna?"

"Maybe someday you will be. But not now. I don't have a job yet. I'll get one, sure enough. But right now we're pretty much on the road ourselves.

"Tell you what, you spend summers with us. We'll come out here and visit the Wilsons. How does that sound?"

It sounded too good to be true, but I knew Bill never lied. If I were with Bill and Edna over the summers, then I could come here and see Jake again, and Rita, and Dora. And there was my new friend, Michelle.

I squeezed Bill's arm by way of answering and said, "What about your agreement with Daddy? The one you told me about?"

"That's another story," Bill said. He fell silent. I knew he didn't want to say more, but I pushed until he did. "Your daddy has funny ideas about doing business," Bill said. "I've known this all along. I didn't think he'd cheat so bad. Nor did Edna. Seems we were wrong. You're better off away, Jamie."

I nodded and said softly, "Maybe so."

"I mean, aside from everything else, the school will have good people who care about kids, about education. It will be a real hard change for you, but you can do it. You're strong."

Hope, like a flower opening in slow motion, each petal stretching away from the center, grew inside me. The hope sat alongside the sadness in my chest. Bill meant what he said. He wouldn't say it otherwise. I knew that about him.

In my mind I saw scattered shards of broken pottery, the kind I'd seen each time Jake and the other kids and I explored a ruin in the Canyon. Like pottery shards, bits and pieces of ordinary life were everywhere. If you took the time to look closely, and maybe dig a little with your fingers in the soil, you could find them. My family was broken into fragments. It wouldn't come together again. It was too late for that now.

"I'll go to the school, Bill, if I get to spend summers with you and Edna."

"It's a deal," Bill answered.

We got on Bill's horse and turned toward camp. On the way back I told Bill about the race with Michelle. "She told me later that she cheated. She admitted it. Then she took me to her camp, and afterward to her secret place in the rocks. I can't tell you were it is, because I promised."

"I guess we all need secret places we can go to, to be by ourselves."

"I want Michelle to be my friend. Jake and Linda think she's a witch. But I don't think that at all."

"The Navajo believe in witches, even if white folks don't," Bill said. "Chances are you're right in thinking she's no witch. She's just an unhappy kid."

I didn't want to talk about Michelle anymore. Instead, I told Bill about my walk in the desert. I told him how I didn't care at first whether I lived or died. I described the millipede and the rattlesnake and the leaf sandals. I told him Dora had described *hozho* to me.

"You understand a little, then, about *hozho*. About how sadness and happiness go side by side? The important thing is to be peaceful in your heart."

"I think so," I answered. "I feel different inside. And Bertha Jim changed. I could tell. Afterward, she sat on the bench under the trees with her fan, and she was much more peaceful than before."

It was late by the time we rode into camp. Everyone was sound asleep. Bill told me goodnight and found a soft, sandy spot near the trees to lay out his sleeping bag.

Before falling asleep, I thought about how much Michelle and I were alike in some ways. She wasn't all wrong to describe us both as outcasts. There was truth, after all, in her words. I decided I wanted to see her before Bill and I left, maybe meet her at the secret cave. I had a yearning to tell her what Bill had said about the boarding school in California.

Early the next morning I went looking for Michelle. I found her a mile downstream, half hidden in the willows, with Norman at her side.

"Bill told me what my parents have decided," I blurted out.

"What do you mean?" Michelle asked.

"I mean, where I go after this, once Bill takes me back home."

"Tell me, then."

I hesitated. Michelle's eyes were glittering in anticipation of what I was about to say. It was the look of a lizard about to pounce on an unsuspecting fly. I wanted to trust her, once and for all. I felt an urgency about telling her what Bill had said. The words finally came. "They're sending me to boarding school in California."

When Michelle heard this, she let out a howl that scared me, and Norman, too. It was a wail. The sound of it reminded me of the freight train whistle outside Gallup.

"Boarding school," she said, in a high quivering voice. I couldn't tell if she was laughing or crying. Her face was turned away from me.

"Bill and Edna said I can spend summers with them and come here, too, for visits."

"And you believe him?"

"Yes."

"How come you believe him?"

"Bill doesn't lie."

Michelle lunged in close to me with her shiny black hair flying as if caught by a sudden breeze. She stared at me. A brutal sneer contorted her face. "You're a baby if you trust anybody."

I felt tears coming, tears of anger. Every time I had it in my head to confide in Michelle, she made sure I was sorry I'd done it.

The two of them ran off quickly. Michelle grabbed Norman's arm and pulled him away. She yanked on him as if he were made of rags. He followed wordlessly.

When I got back to camp, Bill told me we had that day and the next before we'd leave the Canyon.

"Today and tomorrow, that's all?" I asked.

Before Bill could speak, Dora broke in, "We're all leaving pretty soon now," she said. "School starts in a couple of weeks."

"We'll have a feast on your last night," David Jr. said.

"Roast a lamb," David Sr. added.

"Can I get soda from town?" Rita begged, aware that planning a feast meant someone would go to town for supplies. She jumped up and down, tugging at her mother's skirts. "Please, please, black cherry soda?"

"You'll turn into a black cherry if you drink that stuff too much," Jake teased.

"I can have it if I want to," Rita said, scowling at her older brother.

"No arguing," Dora said gently. "There's work to do if we're to have a feast tomorrow night."

My mind was on too many things that morning. I couldn't keep still or pay attention to what people said. I kept thinking about Michelle. What if I didn't see her again for a whole winter?

I think Michelle wanted to see me one more time, too, because when I ran to look for her I didn't have far to go. She was near the Wilson camp, hiding in the willows by the stream. She was alone. For once Norman was not hugging her side.

"When do you go?" she asked. The expression on her face was calm and relaxed.

"Tomorrow."

"So you think he's telling the truth? About you coming back here next summer?"

"Yes."

"I'm going to boarding school, too," Michelle said. She spoke so quietly I had trouble hearing. "In Window Rock."

"Like me," I said.

"No, not like you. White girls go to fancy schools where they let you keep your own name, your religion, everything you own about yourself. It's not like that in Navajo boarding schools."

"You've gone before?" I knew she had, but I asked anyway. I was curious about what had happened there to make her so furious and mean.

"Yes. It made me crazy. They cut my hair and gave me a new name. They wouldn't let me use my real name, the one my mother gave me."

"Is Michelle the name your mother gave you?"

"No. It's the name they chose."

A silence fell between us. I knew she was going to say more, so I kept quiet.

"See, Navajo babies have a Navajo name that's not used out loud, except at special times. You only use it with your family. This way, we feel we are keeping our secrets, our privacy. The Anglo name you get is for everyone else to use. At the boarding school they gave me a third name."

"But why?" I asked, confused.

"They want to make you white. The school is run by

white folks. They want you to fit in with other white people and not be stuck being a Navajo. They want you to use their religion, not the one you were born with."

"What did your own mother call you—I mean, when you were born? What Anglo name did she give you?"

"Emma. It was her name, too."

"Why don't you call yourself Emma?"

"I'm going to now. My Uncle Jeff says he can make them use my real name at the school, not the one they made up."

We began walking toward the Wilson camp. Suddenly Rita and Norman burst out of the underbrush, screaming with glee for having scared us out of our skins.

Michelle laughed. I'd hardly ever seen her laugh. She rushed at Norman as if to capture him. He got away. Rita took my hand and strode by my side. She took giant steps to keep up. After a few minutes, she let go and ran off to find Norman.

That left Michelle and I alone again. She had more to tell me.

"They might try to change you in the new school. Don't let them, or you'll lose your mind the way I did. I felt crazy for a while. Then I got better. My father's brothers, Uncle Jeff and Uncle Joe, understood. They helped me. It was my mother's brothers who brought me snuff when I still needed it. I don't need it any more."

Michelle had never said so much to me at one time. It made me shy to hear her say such important private things. Could I tell her about Daddy? I didn't think so. Not then. Maybe not ever.

"I won't let them change me."

"They'll try. You'll see. They make you feel ugly because you're different."

"I don't care," I said. The words came out in a burst, a small explosion. "I already know I'm different. It doesn't matter what they think, or what they tell me."

"I'm going back because then I can go to college. My father went to college. Remember that time I went to Window Rock? That's where the boarding school is. Uncle Joe took me so we could see if they'd let me back."

She continued, "They said yes, if I promise to be good. I said I'd behave if they let me try for a scholarship to the university in Albuquerque, and if they let me use my real name."

Albuquerque, I thought, *where Mother will live.* "Where is your father? Why don't you live with him?"

"He was killed in a rodeo accident. That's what first made my mother sick—missing him, losing him."

"Do you feel all right about leaving the Canyon?" I asked. "I mean, won't you be homesick at the school?"

"I will always keep coming," Michelle said. "Until I'm as ancient as the old grandmother, Bertha Jim. Nothing will keep me away. I will be buried here."

Michelle swept her hands up through her hair, streaking it with river water. She turned to look at me, saying, "Call me Emma, okay?"

"Okay," I said. "Emma. How'd you get returned to your relatives? After being sold?"

"The tribal government made the white people give me back to my grandparents. Those folks agreed to let me go because they knew where I belonged."

We spent another hour by the river. Before parting, we agreed to be friends. "Come to the Wilson camp tomorrow evening," I said. "There's going to be a big meal in Bill's honor."

"Maybe," she answered. "If you'll remember to call me Emma, maybe I'll come."

"Sure," I said, "Emma."

Every person in the Canyon that I knew, and some that I didn't, came to the feast of roast lamb. The smoke from the cook fires made my eyes sting.

I was surprised to see Michelle—now "Emma"—come slowly through the haze. Norman's hand was gripped firmly in her own.

"Glad you came," I said, smiling.

She nodded and said nothing. She hardly spoke all evening, but she stayed and ate with the rest of us. I noticed that she repeatedly cast shy glances at Jake, as if she expected him to say something to her. He didn't. He was silent Jake that evening. He spoke to no one.

Later, Bill took Emma and Norman back to their camp on his roan. Both of them thought this was silly. They were used to going everywhere in the Canyon, even in the dark. They never thought twice about it. Bill made a joke, saying "What if a mountain lion got you two? It would be my fault, wouldn't it?"

Emma grinned. Her face was dimly lit by the dying fires. "Bye," she said, waving to me from the rump of Bill's horse. "See you next summer."

In the morning, David Sr., Jake, and David Jr. rode to Chinle with Bill and me, to keep us company.

Before we left, I had to say good-bye to the others. Rita cried real tears and clung to me, the way she had often done, with her sticky arms wrapped around my waist.

"I'll see you next summer, I promise." I spoke softly while pushing her bangs away from her forehead. "Behave yourself in kindergarten. You might learn to read this winter. Then you can practice by reading to me next summer."

She nodded, sniffed, gasped for air, and let go.

When I told Dora good-bye, she hugged me and said, "We won't say good-bye. We'll say, 'See you next summer.' "

At the Wilsons' house on the outskirts of Chinle, Bill loaded his horse into the trailer hitched to the pickup. Mr. Wilson and his sons stayed mounted on their horses, forming a semicircle around the truck. I stood by the cab, waiting nervously.

When it was time to say good-bye to Jake, I could not speak. I didn't know what to say or do, and neither did he. We caught each other's eyes and finally Jake said, "Don't forget to come back, after being in California all winter."

"I won't forget," I said.

"California is pretty far away."

"I know, but I'll still be back. I promise."

That was all I knew to say. Jake clearly had no more words. He pulled on the reins of his horse and the animal spun around.

They all started to ride away. The feet of the horses were kicking up dust. Dogs rushed in close to bark and snarl. I wanted to stop the riders, to keep them from going away, to call them back. I felt like screaming the words "Don't go!" But I said nothing.

Suddenly Jake reined in his horse. He turned and loped back to where I stood. "We'll have races next summer," he said. "Maybe you can bring your own horse." He smiled. The sun was bright on his hair. Then he whipped his horse around and galloped off. This time he was waving his arms high in the air, like a rodeo rider, and yipping like a coyote.

I shaded my eyes against the glare and watched until they were out of sight.

Bill drove the pickup into Chinle for a fill-up. He asked me if I wanted a milkshake before we headed out. I answered, "Yes." I hadn't tasted a milkshake since before running away from home.

We stopped in a café that had dusty windows all across the front and a glass door. Inside there were booths with slick yellow seats. The brown plastic tables had shiny tops. Every table had a napkin container, a sugar jar, and salt and pepper shakers. In one corner of the café I saw a jukebox. It was smaller than the kind I knew from home, but otherwise the same.

"Can we play it?" I asked Bill.

He nodded. He told the waitress we wanted two double chocolate malts and some quarters. She smiled and went away. When she came back she had two dollars in quarters and the most delicious-looking milkshakes I'd ever seen.

Bill helped me make the music selections. I chose all the best songs I knew before I ran out of quarters. We sat in our booth after that, not saying anything, listening to the music while we sipped our shakes.

Bill was finished before I was. He went outside to fill the truck with gas while I sat staring through the windows of the café. I watched him and slurped up the last of my shake. I made an embarrassing noise with my straw.

Then I went outside and climbed into the cab to wait for Bill while he checked the oil. He wiped the dipstick with a rag the color of tar.

I was in no hurry to leave that place. And I was glad for the hours it would take us to get back on Highway 66. We'd camp that night in a campground Bill knew about. It was a place we'd camped at before.

I felt like I was about to cross a long suspension bridge between somewhere and nowhere. I saw the shape of Emma's face in the windshield glass. I saw the smile that kept changing with her mood, and her beautiful slanted eyes. I would get where I was going and I wouldn't let them make me into somebody else. They could try as hard as they wanted. It wouldn't work.

Then I thought of Jake and my heart beat faster. Next year he'd be older, just like me. I wondered what he'd be like. Would he grow faster than I did? Would he be an adult man before I was a woman? I crossed my wishing fingers and wished that I would see him every summer until we were both grown.

Bill paid for the gas from a wad of crumpled dollar bills he pulled out of his back pocket. He looked in the direction of the gas station attendant and nodded and touched the brim of his hat before getting into the truck.

Once Bill was in the driver's seat, he slammed the door hard. You had to do that to get it to stay shut. He pushed the brim of his hat up off his brow, exposing the line between his deeply tanned skin and pale white baldness.

He shot me a sideways look and turned the key in the ignition. The engine roared and smoked.

"Ready?" he asked.

"Yup," I said. "Ready."

J